Crossings 27

Puzzle

PUZZLE

Sante Candeloro

Translation by Fred L. Gardaphé

BORDIGHERA PRESS

Library of Congress Control Number: 2020938790

Printed in the United States.

Published by
BORDIGHERA PRESS
John D. Calandra Italian American Institute
25 W. 43rd Street, 17th Floor
New York, NY 10036

CROSSINGS 27
ISBN 978-1-59954-165-5

CONTENTS

I have not written all that I have thought,
but I've thought all that I've written.

Sante Candeloro

INTRODUCTION

A novel is often prepared rationally. Sante Candeloro brushes it with plots, conflicts, and events that make up the life itineraries of its protagonists, many of which were directly experienced by the author. The narrative voice does not acknowledge similarities of any sort during "the years of lead" (the years of political turmoil and social unrest in Italy between 1960 and 1980). His vision of the world invites considerable psychological and ethical examination, if only to give life to a political and civil state without any hypocrisy or ambiguity. A dream!

Eros, rebellion and anger, are expressed in moments of great tension, with words that verge on vulgarity, but which do not refer to any confusion or misunderstanding between the interested parties. Life itself is a series of geometric figures, a puzzle. The title of his novel, therefore, could only be *Puzzle*.

Puzzle is a multicolored jumble of lived cards. The reader, at his or her discretion, can put them together to build a point of view. *Puzzle* does not have a beginning nor an end, at least not as the author has written it. The possible variables belong to those who will read and interpret the most dissimilar and controversial contents. So, it is important to add that this novel is like a matryoshka, Russian nesting dolls. It tells other stories incorporated in its most secret sediments, in the caverns, or in the bright landscapes of a South that is already, in turn, a story told.

Donato Caputo

PUZZLE

It was a Saturday evening in April, one thousand nine hundred and seventy ... and spring had not yet fully arrived. The last storms of the winter were the ones that hurt the most. The winds waved the leaves of the trees and the chimney vanes of the houses. It was early evening, and the frost could be seen in a luminous funnel of the lights behind the street lamps. It seemed like a prelude to a new frost upon everything that was about to be reborn and regenerate.

Near the amphitheater some comrades tried to sell self-published newspapers, some printed, some mimeographed. They were the voices of the alternative press, trying to raise money to forge a counterculture.

We were there to attend the Premiata Forneria Marconi (the Award Winning Marconi Bakery) concert. In front of the box office, many were protesting the high cost of the ticket. After bickering with the managers who did not want to lower the price, someone called the police. Once in place, the officers began to ask for identification documents from all who entered. Some opposed these requests with exaggerated and insistent demands for freedom, such as: "Music is free; it belongs to everyone."

Fortunately, after a negotiation of half an hour among some of us, the police and the concert organizers, calm returned, and we all entered the theater for free. The concert had already begun, and in the public's eyes the enthusiasm could already be read, since at the end of each song, masterly performed, the band received applause. A magic sound filtered through our minds, and the puffed smoke of the joints, until we felt vibrations under the lights of the stage, which often varied in intensity, colors changing with the rising rhythms.

During the break, when all lights came on, my eyes rolled around in search of something ... and in front of me two wonderful blue eyes appeared. Suddenly I moved all of myself into the deep clear of those eyes. Dazed by that splendor, I was incapable of batting an eyelid and of preventing my soul from escaping me. Fear took possession of me. Fear of drowning in that transparency. At that moment I savored a melancholy joy that made me tremble in my bones.

The concert, meanwhile, resumed, and the Premiata Forneria Marconi (P. F. M.) performed "Hans's Carriage," a song where the violin solo, at that moment, was doing the soundtrack to that tangle of looks and eyes that stared at me intently and seemed to say: "I exist!" I let myself be swallowed by the spell of that look!

Beyond those clear pupils, a cascade of thoughts sank into space, like a lightning bolt in a clear sky, and our minds ran on the same frequency at the speed of sound. Both of our thoughts were lost in the void. That woman had noticed me but remained silent, and I attributed all this to the fact that I was fantasizing it all and that perhaps it was all my invention.

At the end of the concert we were still stunned, so much so that we did not notice that the only people left in the theater were the two of us and the roadies packing up the instruments. Imprisoned in each other's eyes, we did not realize that the distance that separated us had ceased to exist. It was she who asked who I was. I remember answering: "I am a common mortal!"

After I answered her like that, there was a long and uninterrupted dialogue between us. We talked about the music and musicians, poets and poetry, art and artists, anarchists and anarchy, philosophers and pacifists. We talked about coups d'état in the countries of the East and Latin America, Africa and Apartheid, and Vietnam. Christ, how we talked! Cold, we walked around the theater, continuing to argue, then someone behind me shouted my name, and I said to her:

"My name is Sebastiano, and you?"

"Maria Clara," she answered.

"I swear that I forgot my friends, and I believe that they were pretty fucked up. By the way, and your friends? "

"For a while now, I prefer to be alone, and don't want to go to concerts with anyone; I want to be alone with myself."

"See you again, if you want."

"Of course. In a month the Nomadi and Guccini concert will be held, and we'll see each other again, at least I hope so. In fact, I will have to prepare some students to pass the third-quarter exams. You know I give private lessons. By the way, I have to prepare myself to take state exams in high school. Pardon my curiosity, but are you a student or a teacher?"

"Neither one nor the other" I answered with a certain humility, adding: "I am a simple carpenter, and I paint canvas and try to sell it." She fascinated me, and looking into her eyes I told her, "Do you know you hypnotized me?"

"Are you serious?"

"It was a good feeling to make my eyes drink the blue of your eyes. But you too have the same feeling. Can you explain why?"

"Maybe…"

"You know, of me there are only so many bones and little meat. I'm not handsome, nor rich. I get by with my clothes, because they are poor and simple, and all this gives me a sad look."

"I know, I noticed, while I watched you, that your sadness is not a mask. Until now, you were the only one to look me in the face. The others, on the other hand, have stared at the space only between my legs."

After she answered me with such sincerity, she waved goodbye, saying I'll see you at the next concert. I walked away and came back to earth.

When they saw me coming, my friends who were waiting began to make fun of me, repeating that I had been late because of that girl, and one of them yelled out, "You got lucky, or am I wrong? Show her the money, and you'll see how that will shake her pussy, otherwise, with a face like yours, she certainly won't give it to you."

Resentful, I replied: "Do you think that you get everything and solve everything with money? What the fuck were you thinking of? You started arguing with the concert managers. That could have ended badly! So why did you want to enter for free when we had the money to pay for the ticket? You think artists shouldn't be paid; they should play for free? How can they get by if they don't earn a living?"

"Look, Sebastiano, you were right with us."

"You put me in the middle, what could I do? As pissed off as you were, I was afraid to take out my money to pay for my ticket. You call yourself friends? Buddies? You who wear rags only to come to concerts, with pockets full of money from fathers who are businessmen, diplomas bought with money. You bust my balls because you see me walking with a girl. I am sick of your philosophizing. If you behave like that, it doesn't matter if your mouths quote radical thinkers; they don't deserve to be in your brains; you are fake champions. I, like a fool, was sorry that my words went against yours, until I was discouraged. I, who have a third-rate sweaty apprenticeship, and you with the high school and the master's degrees, picking on me. Up yours, children of whores."

They climbed into the Renault R4, while I sat on the sidewalk and watched them. The driver braked suddenly when they passed me, and spitting on me, he told me: "If you like misery, you're sitting in the right place. We're going to the pizzeria and then to the whores, and you go back home on foot."

Roaring, they went off singing loudly. After this unfortunate goodbye to my now former friends, I headed home. I returned soaking wet, rain and hail pounding the street, and despite not having the best state of mind, I was relieved that I had told them off.

The next day was Sunday, and I woke up with an unusual state of anxiety. I rolled a joint, and started smoking, then I rolled another. I put the grass back in my jeans pocket, put on my parka, and left the house. I walked a couple of blocks and lit the second joint. I was in a hurry. I was going to the new theater in the public park. I lay down on a stone bench, aiming my smoke rings at their cocks. For a while, I relaxed, and passed the time with my memories. Bad thoughts often pursued old memories, almost to punish them, for they were a part of my existence. There is an unusual effect when trying to empty the mind, the fasting of one's body, when one tries to kill the antagonism between past and present.

My memories didn't need anyone's permission, and they never tiptoed about. They were capricious and cruel, and broke my soul and my balls. Some were as short as February, short and bitter because of the intense cold that emanated. Others were like the wind and the rains of March knocking down the blossoms of almond and cherry trees, leaving the tender and defenseless buds naked. Others were like the sun in July, during the heatwave that started the cicadas singing and watching the sleep of the righteous and the rascals. The memories were like films replayed in slow motion with the eyes of the mind, in bunches they fell like stars during the night of San Lorenzo. My memories were tilting my brain.

I looked around, sitting; the park was filled with people, and the lovers strolled along the avenue holding hands, hugging and kissing each other. The elderly sat on the benches, while I remained alone with my mental saws. Children under the watchful eyes of their parents enjoyed the merry-go-round.

In a daze, I looked without seeing anything in front of me but the dust. I felt the needles of the pines under my shoes, and the frost that had dried, and I heard some pine cones that had fallen on the ground spitting pine nuts, splashing a little everywhere. I was breathing hard. The resin, which dripped from the trunks of the pines, smelled like a light incense, gradually more intense and acrid, and my throat burned. The dust cleared, and the air soaked in incense forced me to cough, and in those moments with the eyes of the mind I saw myself as a child.

In church, people dismounted a catafalque adorned with a black cloth and gilded edge, after a funeral mass had been celebrated. I had arrived early to the catechism lesson because it was my job to arrange the chairs in a circle. Soon, the lesson would begin, and I started to think of the questions that were in the booklet we studied, "Who is God? Where is God?"

Meanwhile the instructor came under the nave of the church, and we listened and learned the prayers by heart. They were to be repeated the day when with a white bow tied to the arm, with clapsed hands we opened our mouths to swallow the body of Christ after confession of sins never committed. I remembered being there, with knees on the ground in front of the priest sitting on a chair, with terror in his eyes, I looked at his big keys. He held them tight in one hand, ready to ring them on my head if he didn't like my answers, while with the other hand he absolved me after having assigned my penance in prayers.

That's when I became a soldier of Jesus and I was rewarded with a watch and a "souvenir photo" with my godfather. I still wonder if it was a caress or a slap to human intelligence, the bishop's hand resting on my cheek.

Then the school, which in addition to sharing the dogmas of the

Church, also inculcated and imparted that slice of corporal repression, using the mouth of the class teacher, who was ready to launch pathetic and repetitive screams if something was wrong. This is his way of teaching, and I remember with bitterness the punishments, the hours that passed slowly. So I ended up kneeling behind the blackboard, after taking my portion of very painful spanks because of the heavy rod that the teacher used. Once I took about twenty, because I had interpreted the theme my way, without respecting the tradition. Compared to another classmate, my punishment was easy. He, not knowing the capital of our region, provoked the teacher who broke his head with a single hit; no doubt he got other beatings when he went home. Today, in all probability, I would not hate the Italian language and its grammatical rules as much as I do if, instead of being punished like that, the teacher had limited himself to simply making me reason my way to understanding.

The land of my deceased grandparents was rich with all kinds of trees, such as cherries, almonds, figs, crabapples, pomegranates, pears, and flowers; behind a rock there was a large prickly-pear plant. Further on, in a ditch, a sinkhole was surrounded by wild weeds. The area, in fact, was a hollow, with several sinkholes called ravines, like the one with the big mouth that gave light to the caves below, a few miles away from the bottom.

The house where we used to go on holiday was small, and there was no electricity. In the evening, my mother lit the oil lamp to illuminate the room. The water well for drinking was outside where a square ended with a young olive tree, not far from an old fig tree. In the only room was a table, some chairs, a cupboard, a bed of two slats and one of three. In the first I slept with my brother and our sister, while in the other my father, my mother, and our little sister. There was a wooden rack, where in the evening the bags stood with figs and tomatoes cut into halves. Farther away, there were wooden planks on which the tomato conserve rested, exposed, drying in the sun all day long. Fava beans were harvested from the dried plants, as well as the chickpeas and lupini, and were deposited in their respective bags, to be transported from time to time by my father to the village on his bicycle's rear fender rack. There also sat bottles of tomato sauce, which we began to produce from the first light of dawn on the square and a concoction from figs. All these provisions were stored on shelves to be consumed during the winter.

We spent all summer producing these stocks, but when it was possible we also went to get something from the landlord whose place bordered ours. His farm included several acres of land. He took care of chickens, rabbits, sheep, pigs, cows for milk and cheese, and hens for eggs. He had a donkey, a horse, two wagons, some cats, and a docile dog that held out his paw as a sign of affection when you tried to pet it. The place was big, and the landlord rented a few rooms to vacationers. This was a district known as "The Indians," because during the Second World War a detachment of the Allied troops from India had camped there. The vacationers, in turn, in addition to the premises of the landlord, often occupied other homes, crowded the whole district. As a result, all of them together began to form a small army. We gathered together in the evening, each one singing his favorite song, in an area set aside for the occasion now in one place, then in another, outside their respective homes. The songs were accompanied by the clapping of hands, and the banging of pots and two aluminum lids. The pot was battered by two wooden spoons that our parents used in the kitchen. The two lids were clapped together, often out of time, because it was the first time for someone; they all had fun that way.

The landlord had three children. Two were male adults, one in the military and the other responsible for the business in other districts. Tonietta, on the other hand, was the last of the three children, and at the age of fifteen, took care of the farm. She had short boy-like hair and brown eyes. She usually wore the same dress, made from the unstitched skirts of her mother and refashioned for her fawn-like body, and she used to walk barefoot.

Her parents were greedy and stingy, and everything they got from the sale of their goods was set aside for the sake of accumulating money, while exploiting their daughter for all the tasks. They deprived her of an education to get her used to hard domestic work and livestock care. The mother took care of the work of the farm with her daughter, while the father plowed the fields. He stopped at the various cheese factories in the country, filling up cans, then went to the fruit and vegetable market, collecting produce, and from the restaurants he picked up the leftovers from the kitchens. On his return, he poured what was transported into a vessel, adding acorns harvested earlier in the small groves that embellished the land. Tonietta, drawing the slop from the vessel with a bucket, fed the pigs, and one Sunday I helped her carry those buckets to the pigsty. She opened the gate, we entered, and as she poured the contents into a large pile, the pigs grunted as they approached to begin feeding themselves.

Tonietta, on her return, clung to a large trunk to collect figs from the highest branches, where they were more mature and sweet. I took advantage of my position under the tree to take a peek, looking at the panties that shone between her thighs, and for the first time, became so excited that my bird stood up. She, moving sensuously in her scurrying among the branches, soon after came down from the tree and said: "The figs aren't ripe yet."

It was almost evening, and my parents had gone to town to attend Sunday Mass with the rest of the family. At home I was alone, and Tonietta's thighs and panties came back to my mind. I had an erection again, and my bird, still virgin, bristled as I began to tighten it in my hands. On one hand, I felt pain, and on the other, a feeling of pleasure, and with a consistent quick up and down, the cherry that forced me to piss shortly afterwards. Meanwhile it burned me and didn't want to go back to its place, so I rushed home, and with a rag soaked in olive oil I moistened the tip, and finally everything went back to where it was before the erection.

Weekdays I rode my bicycle to the shop and so could only join in the evening singing with the children of the vacationers, including Tonietta. On Sundays, I read in the shade of a tree or worked. That Sunday, I dug up the ground, laying the stones in a tub, which when full I would grab the handle and carry it to the heap of stones. I heard a roar of a motor approaching, and then suddenly it stopped. I knew what it was. I left the tub and immediately ran to the farm. Marcuccio was standing in front of his vintage scooter; two racks were placed on top of one another. In the one below, there were chickens and hens, while the other was empty. Around him there was a group of children who were my playmates, including Tonietta accompanied by her parents. I approached them as they talked and Marcuccio casually opened the door of the cage on top and lowered his hand inside, pulling out the only tenant in that cage. I had never seen a rooster so beautiful. Marcuccio boldly introduced him to us and to the chickens and proudly said: "Behold, it is the new king, young and strong; from the old man will come a broth. From tomorrow on you will see how many eggs there will be!"

He had negotiated the price with the sparring man, until he sold it to him and he placed the rooster in his new harem. The housewife, not convinced, said to her husband: "You paid too much," and the stiff husband answered her: "Did you want it for free? Did you see that marvelous animal Marcuccio brings us?" After a short pause, he added: "Now, do me a favor. Go into the kitchen, check the fire under the big earthenware sauce, and as you go there, fill the saucepan with water and light the other fire, I'm getting hungry." Then he lit a cigar and walked away.

Tonietta, after her mother had gone into the kitchen, opened the sack of corn, took a bucket, sank it, and skillfully pulled it out full to the brim. Then, with gusto and joy, she tossed it over the ground, where the old and the new rooster with hens and chickens pecked at it all.

My companions and I, as though it was a game, in single file, followed Tonietta who continued to toss the corn. After she had finished her work, the youngest of us went home to have lunch, while the older ones stayed to keep her company. To protect ourselves from the rays of the sun we went under the wagon tent, and from here we looked at the horse, tied to the trunk of the red mulberry and eating food from the bag hanging from its harness. Suddenly he started to whinny, shaking; we laughed when we noticed that he had begun to piss. We were enchanted by his member, that looked like a rolling pin that eventually disappeared between his thighs. Tonietta laughed, and said that the pig's prick looked like a corkscrew, while that of the bull was almost as long as that of the horse, but the tip was as smooth as an acorn and as thick as a pinecone. She knew all these things, because she told me that the year before, Gasparino appeared to bring one for the heifers, and she secretly observed the scene of the mounting. At the end of this conversation, everyone left, and only Tonietta and I remained.

"I'll wait for you in the barn around milking time." After telling me this, she went back to her duties. I returned home where I found the table set for lunch. My mother told me that as soon as I finished eating I would finish the removal of the stones, and then I would go to Vituccio to do the same, since I had promised to do it the previous Sunday. In the afternoon, as planned, I was in the back, and with a shovel in my hand I gathered stones, while Vituccio took his nap under the veranda. I had almost filled the sack when he suddenly woke up. Still half sleepy and moving his jaws, he said: "Bravo, I'm happy with your work." Then he turned away and I followed him.

He entered the house, a sort of open shed where anyone could see what was inside. When he arrived in that half-disordered room, he opened a deep old chest, and bending down, grabbed something with his hands. They were books. He put them on a floor where there was paper, then he pinched a piece of paper and wrapped the books, and turning he said to me, "This gift is the reward for your work. Thank you."

Happily, I put the bundle of books under my arm and went home. It was already late afternoon, when my father asked me: "What's under your arm?"

"Some books Vituccio gave me," I answered with satisfaction.

"Let me see," he said in amazement. I handed him the package. He unwrapped it, and while he was looking at the cover of the first book, he started swearing, and then he told me: "This garbage still exists? Throw them in the fire!"

I obeyed, but before doing so I wanted to know why those books had made my father so agitated. They were scholastic texts of the Fascist period. I burned them and went to the farm where I saw Tonietta already milking her cow.

She wiggled its udders with skill, and the milk shot down into the bucket below; she did this every afternoon, at the same time, since her brother took care of the milking in the morning. Once the bucket had been filled, she grabbed it to take it to the adjoining room where she poured it into a larger container, covered it with a towel, and returned to the stable. She had noticed me, but pretended not to have seen me, and when she finished milking, she aimed her bright eyes at me and said: "Come, let's go to the barn."

The entrance was where a ladder led to a window. It was the opening to the loft that served as a barn. She climbed the steps, and I had the modesty of not looking at her thighs from under her skirt, and when she came to the window, I was still halfway up the rungs. Then I joined her, and together we went inside, where she found the pitchfork and began to throw the hay down at the animals through a trapdoor above the great manger. I looked around, and noticed farming tools on the wall, the gear for the horses and a saber in its sheath. I asked Tonietta what it was for, and she said "It was my grandfather's; he was a carabiniere." Then she added surprisingly: "Take two bags and lay them on the ground where there is no more hay, because we must do a job together."

Leaving the pitchfork, and taking one step away from me, she said: "Will you show me?"

"What?" I replied.

"Your bird."

"Oh!"

"Do you have one, or not?"

"Yes, but I'm ashamed."

"Have you ever played doctor?"

I remained embarrassed and she, pressing me even more, told me: "Pretend you have to piss. Come on, do it." She ordered me while she pulled up her clothes; she didn't wear panties. For the first time I saw mother nature covered by the hair of puberty, and excitedly I tried to piss. In doing so, she looked at me, and astonished told me: "It's still closed." I, in fear of pain, stroked myself with care until the cherry came out, and finally pissed. She grabbed it, and as she stroked it, he stood up. With joy she was pulling me up and down, then suddenly, as she stopped, she crouched in front of me, lay down on the sack, took my hand and placed it on her pubis. Instead, she began to touch the inside of her thighs with it, until she stuck a finger in the small opening trying to move it inside. Warming up and inviting me to play that game, she told me: "Put your finger inside, and feel how warm it is." She didn't have to ask twice, and when I stuck my finger, I told her: "It's not hot. Wow, it is hot!" Grabbing my wrist, she led my finger and pushed it inside and pulled it out, in rhythm that shifted to a fast pace as she moaned in pleasure. With my other hand, I stroked her breasts like plums and nipples like lentils, and kissed them. After a while she stopped, and I was stoned with the upright bird. Instead, she relaxed and stretched out completely, and said: "Nothing came out of the pea."

Confused and red in the face, I tried to put the cherry back inside. Only then did I realize that it was covered by a watery gelatin, which was not urine. Tonietta, after enjoying me, warned me, and told me:

"Don't say anything to anybody. What we have done will always be our secret."

"Agreed. Tell me, though, where did you learn to do these things? "

"Do you know that couple of vacationers who had those children who were always fighting each other? One afternoon he very carefully washed the floor under the veranda, and soon after I had finished my labors, I heard moans coming from a window. I came closer, and I saw the couple in a naked exchange. His wife held her husband's cock in her hand, and played with it, like a cow's nipple, only a little longer and at the tip there was a large acorn. From the way she squeezed it, it had to be really hard, so much so that she put it in her mouth and sucked it, licked it. Then she knelt like a sheep, and, from behind, he stuck it in her vagina, and with his hands around her hips pulled her to him and pushed her away. Easing his grip, and with one hand on her neck, he pushed her head down until her face touched the sheets. Then he caught her breasts that hung in his hands, and stroked them, while the bird in the vagina flew back and forth faster and faster until the moment when, exhausted, they fell back on the bed. He, turning on himself, touched his cock, then jumped up, and approached the window. He seemed to be carrying something in his hands. I had time to hide behind the column of the concrete pillar of the veranda, and

I saw something land near me that the man had thrown out of the window. I waited as he came back into the room, then cautiously I went to look in the oleander bush for the object I had seen falling over there. I found it lying on a branch, and it was a transparent balloon soiled with glue.

"A few days later I saw my brother in his room with his pants and underpants lowered, standing looking at the wall and stroking his cock and doing alone what I had seen the couple do. After several tugs, a dull white liquid leaped from his cock and fell to the floor. Then he walked over to the wall, and took something off, and bending down, he cleaned the floor thoroughly. When I made up his room, about half an hour later, I lifted the mattress and found a folded sheet of newspaper. I opened it, and a naked woman appeared. At that moment I understood where the glue had come from, which I had also seen in the balloon I found on the oleander."

I was surprised, and I was about to say something to her, but she interrupted me, and added: "I beg you, keep this all secret; if they find out there'll be a fierce beating for me. Already my mother warned me at the beginning of the year, when I showed her my panties stained with blood. She smiled at first, then became serious, and told me: "You are now a young lady, and you are ready to have children. Woe to you, if you get touched by males, and if you get pregnant, you can forget about me and your father. You go straight into the grove to eat acorns and sleep under the trees.

"Now listen; come back, always during milking hours. Climb the ladder and wait for me in the barn."

The following Saturday the boss closed for vacation and rented a room at the sea for him and his family. I had never been to the sea; nobody had ever taken me to a beach. Nicola, one of the workshop workers, promised to take me on the back of his Lambretta scooter. So, the next day, sitting behind him and grabbing his sides, we set off along the coast. At the edge of the Lambretta I looked from one side of the road, then the other side, seeing pine and cypress trees flow in reverse, as well as the dry, stone walls that divided the fields. When we reached our destination, we stopped in front of a monastery built out of heavy volcanic rock, from where there grew some caper plants, and at its feet there were fig trees. For centuries its majesty watched over the nearby coast, poor in sand with many boats.

Excited by that sight, I jumped off the Lambretta and ran towards the nearest opening. I looked for some sand, and here at last, almost trembling with joy, I put my feet in the water for the first time. The water on the shore was transparent, under the rocks was darker, then dyed with deep blue, and on the horizon was a huge celestial screen; it was heaven! The sea felt cool on my thighs; I caught some water, and with a cup made from my hands, I wet my face and my hair in a frenzy, breathing its scent. The fishermen, meanwhile, unloaded the fish caught overnight. The customers stood on the rocks, waiting for the fishermen to arrive, ready to buy. On my left, there was a building with a veranda that served as a shop where you could find everything from ice cream to bread, fried fish, and roasted octopus.

On the other side of the shop, there were the vacation homes just a few steps from the sea. Here I ran into some friends from school who ignored me. In an open space below the monastery, where I had been since I arrived, stood an elderly gentleman who wore a white vest and a red scarf tied around his neck, and he played the guitar singing "La Bicicletta" in the Barese dialect. A crowd of people urged him on, while he, taking a break, popped a bottle of cold beer, and smashed it, after drinking it; imitating Totò, he mimed the explosions of the fireworks, accompanying himself with sounds, as if they were crackling firecrackers. Gathering applause from those present, with eyes lit with joy and with humility, he thanked them by bowing. Then he greeted everyone, slung his guitar over his shoulder, got on his bicycle, and returned to his village, which was also mine. I knew him, in fact, having seen him do his little shows in the country's districts, and I knew his name was Nanuccio.

Nicola decided to leave. That morning, on the Lambretta, we traveled much of the Adriatic coast, stopping occasionally on other beaches full of bathers. At noon we returned, and having got off the scooter, I handed him the bag of mussels and octopus he had bought from a local stall. I thanked him for the beautiful morning that he let me spend, wishing him good holidays, and under the sun I returned home. In the afternoon I went to the appointment I had with Tonietta in the barn. I saw her get nervous already coming up the stairs, and when she stood beside me, she said to me: "I had my period again."

"All right, don't worry too much. I'll stay with you anyway, and help you collect the hay."

"You'd better not. Nervous as I am, I run the risk of acting badly towards you. See you next Sunday."

"All right, I'll be there." I left the barn and went back to the hollow alone.

That week the vacationers diminished because some families went to sea to spend the August holiday. Alone in the background, not knowing what to do, I took the books from the box, and leafed through some of them. Later, I remembered that I had taken from the shop a piece of plywood as big as a sheet of sketchbook. I took a pencil and tried to copy the *Grande Blek* comic book. The passion was there, but the result was disappointing. Not happy, I turned to the plywood, trying again. It was even worse than before. Angrily, I took the sandpaper and scraped it. Once I had more or less erased the earlier marks, I was designing a country house and almond trees that succeeded with dignity, but they were in every way scribblings compared to one of my peers. I envied those sketches drawn with talent, and in of this state of mind I scraped my plywood several times to draw again. Tired of this pastime, I started to go around the district to collect blackberries from the brambles on the bush, a little as I did earlier in the morning. I was going to pick prickly pears with a small jar of sauce that managed to fit right over the spiny fruit, and pulling, I was able to pluck it from the plant, and dropped it in a bucket. At home I added water and left them to rest. After about ten minutes, with a knife I took one and with three quick swipes on the full-bodied peel, the fruit came out, and each person there, extending a hand, carried the fruit to his mouth tasting its flavor.

One night, unable to sleep, I thought of Tonietta, her little shell of flesh that titillated me, and her eyes lighting up with pleasure as I did. I remembered the panting of her breath, which reached a climax, the suddenly waned. Tonietta, free, uninhibited, simple, and wild! My penis stood for a while, then suddenly emptied without my touching it.

I, like a fool, thought of all those cone-shaped cards I shot from my blowgun (it was my mail post) to Giuliana when she came out of the church. She read the notes and smiled in agreement, but never came to meet me. What hypocrisy! Tonietta, on the other hand, whom I had not asked for anything, had opened the gate to her Eden, letting me enter inside, if only with a finger.

I went to the farm on Friday of that week; Cosimo stopped there with his motorcycle loaded with a galvanized case, and inside were anchovies and sardines immersed in ice and covered with a waxed cloth. To weigh the fish he carried a small steelyard scale made from a brass plate fixed to the bar by different chains. Tonietta's parents, and even my mother, bought some fish.

I stood behind Tonietta, when I saw that suddenly she stroked her buttocks. Uninvited, with one hand she made an eyelet, and with the other she slid her middle finger, imitating a sexual act. Placing her hands forward, she turned to me and with her mouth she mimed her request to go to the barn on the following Sunday. I had faith in her invitation, and when we were together in the hayloft, side by side, we were discovered by her father who had gone up to the barn to look for something. He beat us for a good reason, and when I returned home, my parents, already informed of what happened, also beat me.

The following Monday the boss reopened the shop after the holidays, and I, still aching and with various bruises on my face, resumed my work explaining my absence with an excuse.

Work began with a fight between Nicola and Ugo, who wanted to be the young boss. Ugo got it because the master had sided with him. Nicola, out of spite, quit work. He was sure he would find work at another shop, because he had the skill, and then, he needed to, since every month he had payments to make for the purchase of the Lambretta. Five of us remained in the shop: the boss, Ugo, Michele, Saverio, and me. Ugo had a bad temper, and wasn't as good as Nicola, but became a young boss because he was a pimp. He did not call the others by their names, instead he used dirty and offensive nicknames. In addition, he ordered us to buy things for him: from the newsagent the magazine *Tex and Nembo Kid*, from the grocer a sandwich, from the fountain to get water, and tobacconists for ten cigarettes at a time. Finally, he wrote numbers on the smooth sandpaper facade, and instructed some of us to go to the lottery desk to play the lotto numbers listed on the Wheel of Rome.

"Who knows," he once said "maybe the Pope might help me to hit a winner."

The boss, an old man, was irascible. He sang, however, when he was in a good mood, sacred hymns and church songs. Often, with the wood plane in motion that served as an orchestra, one could hear him throughout the neighborhood. In his absence, and when Ugo wasn't there, we also sang. Our orchestra, however, was made of poor instruments, like hammer blows on nails, screwdrivers, and chisels that drummed on plywood bottoms of drawers turned for resonance as if they were tambourines. One day Ugo, who knew about our songs, asked me if I knew the song "Marina." I said yes, and he replied: "Today, when you finish eating, you have to bring this letter to Sisina. Be careful not to let yourself be discovered, and then bring me the answer."

In the afternoon I went to the neighborhood where Sisina lived, and as soon as I took the road, I began to sing "Marina." The path took me into the hollow, and I sang until I reached front of Sisina's house, where I waited for her to come out onto the balcony. In a little while, she opened the window and looked out onto the street and saw me. Lightning quick, I took the note out of my pocket, attached it to a clothespin, and threw it to the balcony. She picked it up, read it, and nodded her approval, immediately going back in. Glad to have completed the task assigned to me by Ugo, I was leaving again, when suddenly water came down on me, and I heard a voice shouting: "Get out of here, go and sing to your sister, you delinquent you."

When I reached the shop, Ugo immediately asked me how it had gone. I told him that Sisina had responded positively. Taking a better look at me, Ugo added: "Did anyone see you? Wasn't Giuditta the foreman there, who has a tongue like a scissors and eyes everywhere?"

"How would I know?"

"You goof! Couldn't you sing the song softly?"

"She wouldn't have heard me; don't worry, no one saw me while I was throwing the clothespin with the note onto Sisina's balcony."

Then spreading the palm of my hand under his eyes, I thought he was giving me the money he had promised me. He did not move, and moreover told me: "In the absence of the boss you three must do as I say."

Meanwhile the other two colleagues of mine entered, and while he told me to cut the sandpaper, he ordered them: "You prepare the glue. You take clamps and crossbars that we have to glue to those four looms, and you," turning back to me "useless prick, remember tonight to go to the fountain and get the water you have to bring to the master's house"; not happy, he said again: "As for the money I promised you, you can forget about that."

He teased me, that asshole. I was crying, and sobbing I thought I could no longer buy a number of the prairie series that contained the adventures of Grande Blek and Captain Miki.

I recalled the note to Sisina on which Ugo had written: "Come to the station on Sunday morning, at half past nine, or I'll leave you. I'll be waiting for you between the fifth and the sixth pile of beams."

What a fucking asshole! He also blackmailed his girlfriend. For the whole week, Ugo broke our balls, me in particular, adding: "If you have dirty hands, go to wash them; you have to hold my dick when I piss" and boldly told me: "Bring me your cousin, and you'll see how I can be. The next time you ask me permission to go to the bathroom, I'll have you squashed, I will not send you, and if you try pissing on the sawdust, I'll beat you silly." That bad imitation of Elvis Presley could do something like that, and he told me with his mouth frothing and blood in his eyes. Trembling with fear, I swore my revenge.

On Sunday morning, during the children's Mass, I took off. The train station had a surrounding area where there was a stack of railroad ties. They took up almost the entire free area, and the rows were superimposed on each other; corridors wound between the piles. In addition to the tracks, half a meter high, there were steel wires, set on short iron poles with pulleys, which started from the ticket office and finished at the level crossing. Beyond the wires that skirted the tracks, there were trees, lindens, poplars, and elms. In this area there was an escarpment overgrown with weeds and ferns, which ended in a sinkhole for collecting rainwater. Around the latter, the little bit of land was surrounded by a system of dry stones that formed a terraced vegetable garden, over which stood a huge oak tree. Going up the side facing the oak, an old distillery sat in an open space. Among its vast sheds abandoned for years, a Sylvan pine guarded the ruins like a centurion.

All this was a short distance from the stacked cross-pieces, where I stood on the poles, stretched out and piled up like a pyramid. From there, I pierced a hole through a carton, stuck my head inside, and looked through the tiny window. Someone looking at that cardboard could take it for it for an open box, thrown there by accident.

Camouflaged, I kept watching, until I saw Ugo inspecting the area; as he approached the posts, I feared the worst. Fortunately, it was not so, because he picked up a discarded fruit box and took it with him to the corridor where he had agreed to meet Sisina; there he sat down and waited for her to come. He didn't wait long. The station master, crossing the tracks, went to turn the crank to guard the passage of the train by lowering the bars, with the *dlen dlen* sound of the propellers moving on the rod. The slowing train passed in front the piles to enter the station and stop, so that the travelers could get off; then it left, and the station was empty.

Suddenly, Sisina came out quickly and was already near the meeting place. Long braided black hair, a white polka-dot blouse, and a blue skirt with a petticoat, gave her the air of a dancer. Counting the piles she found the right one, and slipped inside. They began to swallow each other quickly. Ugo unbuttoned her blouse and pulled out her big, firm titties, and started to lick and suck them. Sisina pulled down the zipper of his blue jeans, took his already hard cock and rubbed it between her tits overheating him even more. Excited, Sisina brought it to her mouth, closing her full lips, then opening them again, passing her tongue around the glans, sucking it for a few minutes. Ugo, blind with pleasure, with Sisina's head between his legs, bent over her shoulders to grab her behind and lift her skirt, and admired her panties. He pushed her forward; she opened her legs wide, and making his way up he put the trophy between her thighs, much to her enjoyment. After that, he got her to stand on the box, took her panties off, knelt in front of her and with his head under her skirt he probably moved his tongue in the shell covered by a grove of hairs. Having done that, he took her out of the box, sat her down, and put the member back in her mouth, between her tits, back in her mouth and on her tits, and in a frenzy, ejaculated. He stopped, not wanting to, and out of spite slapped Sisina's tits; then with a handkerchief he wiped her face and sent her off, keeping her panties for himself.

Sisina sobbing, ran, fading away from my little cardboard screen from where, crouched, I had witnessed their games. I backed my head from the window, left the posts, took the blowgun I had put in the back pocket of my jeans, loaded it with a cone, and blew as hard as I could, shooting it in the direction of the tracks. The cone, flying, drew an arc in the sky. It was the signal that my buddies were waiting for. Suddenly, on the top of the two piles where Ugo was intent on tidying up, little buckets and bags appeared. They were full of dirty water and dirt, and my friends launched them, hitting Ugo. Wet and nervous, he came out cursing and threatening, but by then my friends had already disappeared along the slope, and he was helpless. I laughed and thought that that morning, with my neighborhood friends, we had behaved like the protagonists of the novel *I Ragazzi della Via Pal.*

I went to the bar, where my father left his work tools, took the bicycle, and took a box filled with comic books from his luggage rack. It was the pay for my friends, with whom I had seen the first sex film in which the main character had been hit with a water balloon. Happy for the revenge accomplished, I went to church.

The Mass was over, and the faithful came out in droves. I ran into the sacristy where the priest was taking off his vestments and whispered to the altar boy asking what was the color of the stole with which the priest had officiated. Giannetto told me and we both left through the front door.

In the empty square was my boss, who stopped me and commanded me to run some errands. I ran into my father as I passed the barbershop and he asked me about my presence at Mass; lucky for me that I was standing in front of the church at that time. With a warm heart, and wings on my feet, I went to get my bike from the room. I thought that Ugo, suspecting me, had asked the teacher where I was.

I rode to the hardware store, where I bought a sheet of black cotton and a bottle of spirits. With this stuff I went first to the master's house where his wife gave me an old linen lining. Then to the house of Mastro Luccio and I told him to come to the shop with the necessary goods, since someone had died, and the coffin chosen by the relatives had to be polished. Once in the shop, I helped the master to place the coffin and lid on the wooden horses and sprinkle it with linseed oil. Mastro Luccio arrived with the basket full of shellac and paint bottles. The box was dry, and noticing it, he took the apron and put it on. Then he began to prepare a black cotton pad covered with squared linen; he soaked it with liquid shellac from one of the bottles, and began to polish, whistling a theme for a funeral march; by noon he finished the first coat, and leaving everything on the horses, went to lunch at his house and then returned in the afternoon. Each of us did the same. At home, my mother asked me the color of the stole the priest had worn. I told her, but she was not happy, and asked me what the priest said during the homily. I answered her: "Who can understand that with all those Latin words he says?"

"Really, you always were and will be a dimwit." Then she added: "Did you know that Ugo came looking for you; I told him you were at mass. What does that guy want from you? You tell me he mistreats you, and then he comes looking for you? Who can understand it all?"

We sat down at the table and finally had lunch. At the shop that afternoon, the two masters had already resumed work, and immediately, as I arrived, they sent me to the tinsmith to ask how his work with the zinc sheets was going. I also went to the dressmaker, to see how she was doing with the satin. In the evening, everything was ready (polished, dry, and decorated with zinc and silk). We placed the pillow and fixed the cover with screws. Finally, the coffin was loaded atop the cart, and we brought it to the house of the deceased. Unfastening the ties, I turned my head, and saw on the town's public announcements wall the poster that reported his death. When we reached the front door, we noticed that they had already laid the black cloth over the lintel. I took the cover off the coffin, and some onlookers carried it upstairs where the corpse was placed inside. The cover was placed upright against a wall of the room. Lit candles were placed at the four corners of the catafalque, surrounded by crying relatives.

The next day the boss sent Ugo and my colleagues to mount windows to a building. Then, turning to me, he said: "Get the toolbox ready, put the shop in order, and wait for the funeral at the dead man's house."

Seated on a balcony of an outside staircase, I saw the cushions and crowns of palms and flowers coming. I saw the confreres of the sacred congregation together with the Franciscan novices, the orphans with the nuns of the charitable institute, and, finally, the carriage with the coachman dressed with a top hat. The coachman, fumbling with the reins, parked the carriage in front of the entrance. Four angels had been carved on the corners of roof, and the carriage was drawn by two black horses with a plume blocked with leather straps between the ears and black blinders blocking their side vision. Meanwhile the band members and the priest had arrived with the altar boys in tow, and behind it all, my boss who was beckoning me to join them. We went up to the house and after the prayers, my boss grabbed the cover leaning against the wall to close the coffin with the screws amid the screams of relatives. They carried it down, and the coffin was placed on the carriage; just after this, the band also moved and began to perform the first of the many funeral marches that would be played throughout the procession. My boss, in the meantime, ordered me to wait for him at the cemetery, and that he would follow the funeral to check that everything went smoothly between the church and the arrival at the cemetery. Under the cypresses at the cemetery's entrance gate sat two old women, seated on chairs, reciting prayers on behalf of the souls of the dead who requested them in exchange for small donations. The two old ladies politely asked me, "Who is the deceased?"

"His name is Attilio, and he was the ax master."

"Oh, what a good person. He is a good soul and will almost certainly go to heaven." "What did he die of?" added the other old woman. "How old was he?" "Did the daughter-in-law who argued with him come to the funeral?" asked the first.

"He was eighty years old" and I did not add anything else, because I had wasn't sure if he indeed was "A good soul, and whether or not paradise deserved him."

After a long time, the funeral procession arrived at the cemetery, and on the pallbearers' shoulders the coffin was led to the chapel not far from where the priest celebrated the last annointing. Immediately after, the tinsmith welded the zinc lid. My boss and I put the screws in their holes, tightened them, then closed the coffin with the lid upon which some bunches of flowers were still tied. Before the cemetery workers brought the coffin to its niche, the master had me disassemble the four wooden feet and the cross, and the relatives after the condolences in tears accompanied the coffin before the burial plot. I returned from the graveyard with the cross on my shoulders and the toolbox I had used. Passing by the house of the deceased, I saw the comings and goings of people holding pots covered with tea towels in their hands. They served u cuônze, the consoling lunch for those returning after the burial of the body.

In the shop, I hung the cross on the beam of the wall, and pulled back the curtain. I opened one of the roughed-out coffins and placed in it the four lion-shaped feet. Putting everything back into place and opening a door of a cabinet, I took out a basket that contained a bottle of oil, some pasta, and some bundles of flour. It was another task that had to be carried out by order of the master, and with the shopping bag, I set off with my bicycle to the recipient's house, who, as soon as he noticed me from the balcony, yelled at me for being late.

"I could not come sooner. The master is still at the cemetery."

"If only he would stay there forever," she replied, pulling on her shopping bag with the rope. I did nothing and went back to the shop waiting for the master to return.

More weeks passed and the harvest season began in all the districts. There was not a farm or a place in the village that did not have a winepress and the vats where the grapes were pounded barefoot. Since the day I had taken the barrel to the barn, I had not been able to talk to Tonietta, as her guards watched her closely, and now they took her with them to the harvest.

I got up early in the morning and climbed up a high wall. Hidden behind the bushes, I waited for the passage of the tractor. This time I was lucky. I saw her standing on the tractor driven by her father. The mother and brother sat beside him on a board that served as a seat. Everyone faced away from him, and at every jerk of the tractor he jiggled between the empty crates. The tractor took a downhill road, and I left my hiding place to make myself noticed. Her head was shorn like a sheep, and yet it remained enchanting, dazed, I blew her a kiss and she blew one back. As the cart pulled away, I cried, thinking that rather than harvesting, Tonietta was being taken to the Boario market.

In those days we moved to the village. My father had already whitewashed the house which smelled of fresh lime and was ready for our stay throughout the winter. My brother and I went to the barber for haircuts, paid for by our father. Our mother, in turn, bought two new, white smocks for our two little sisters, Stellina and Domenica, who would be entering kindergarten. I went out to the barber, and while my brother was coming home, I went to the municipal library to return the book, *The Boys of the Via Pal*, which I had borrowed. On the way home, I thought to myself of all that had happened in such a short time. Only then did I realize that ignorance and innocence had taken the path of no return, slamming the door of malice in my face. It was a few days before the start of the school year, and I was worried because in the afternoon I had to continue going to work. I reflected on my future, where my two commitments appeared to be the school and the shop. On these last thoughts both childhood and carefree days seemed to me to be marked forever by a single word: *end*.

The school holidays had flown nonstop and warm like the shadows. The black smock with the white collar and the usual blue bow was a distant memory for me. I had grown up too fast, not being able to account for what was happening around me. At school, a storm of hormones was unleashed within me among the *Iliad*, the *Odyssey*, and the *Divine Comedy*. Beyond these classics, I read *Lady Chatterley's Lover* and *Lolita*. Secretly in class, black-and-white porn photos passed from hand to hand, and so each of us opened his imagination to every sequence of kamasutra, only to find himself "drowned" in the pocket hole. I wasn't studying so I missed the discussions of mathematics and other subjects. I really was a *capotosta*. In spite of it all, I graduated, barely passing all subjects.

The following summer we did not take a vacation because the land of my grandmother's house been inherited by my mother's brother. In the shop worked Master Andrea, Ugo, I, and nobody else, since no parent had offered his son up for apprenticeship. With Ugo, I often quarreled, and since the day of the balloon episode, he was angry because he could never find a clue that would connect it to me. That story had turned him into a beast, and he took his revenge by making me do the complicated jobs that he didn't like.

Some emigrants abroad I knew who were on holiday told me their stories. Fascinated by those stories, I thought that if I emigrated, I could make money like them. I had an uncle in France, who was on vacation, and I took the opportunity to go with him to find his fortune in those parts. Once there, I did not find a job because I was still a minor, and after only three months, I had to return home, paying back the money for the train ticket.

After failing this attempt, Master Andrea took me back to work because Ugo had been fired a few weeks before. I had lost track of my schoolmates and neighborhood; everyone had made his choice either continuing his studies or leaving the country forever. I was messed up. I tried many things, but nothing worked. I also tried to study guitar, but I encountered enormous learning difficulties. With the girls, I tried my best, and felt bad when each affair ended. To distract myself, I began to collect records, which together with new friends, I listened to on a turntable of a club that we had furnished, splitting the rental costs. There were few girls and they refused to dance with me, so I consoled myself by dee-jaying; when the requests were unavailable, I often ending up bickering with the couples who danced.

On Sundays with these new friends, I would go to the beach by bus, and we would bring along the record player; we ruined it because of the grains of sand that it kept swalllowing. Those who knew how to swim performed dives from the highest rock; we, and others around us, cheered them on, proud of our friends. In the evening, along the road leading to the municipal villa of our country, we wore our best clothes and walked to the bar in the piazza located in the park of the villa. Here a jukebox gulped down coins and threw up songs, and we, with our eyes out of their sockets, looked at the legs of girls with shorter skirts. All the guys chose a corner or a tree behind which to hide and masturbate.

One night at the club, I met a new friend, Carlo, a few years older than me, and after hearing me sing the song on the turntable, suggested I join his band. He took me to his house, and pulling a case out from under the bed he opened it and showed me a Fender electric guitar. He connected the plugs to their holes and with the pick and a lot of skill he performed *La Casa del Sole*, demonstrating skills in the arpeggios highlighted by an amplifier. At the end of the song he asked me if I was available to join his band. I accepted willingly, and after the second trial, I was participating in the weddings at which the group performed. Mastro Andrea, however, did not like this, because every now and then I gave up working in the shop to follow the group that, instead, gave me nothing. In fact, I sang only when their first singer was tired, and mine, after all, was just a presence, just there for fun. This story did not last long, and the popular songs to learn by heart were coming from singing shows of Sanremo, the Summer Disco, the Cantagiro, the Festival Bar, and many others. The group was forced to imitate the new songs the audience demanded because they had heard them on the Hit Parade. This commitment began to bore me, because instead of singing the songs that we liked and were passionate about, we had to perform specific requests. I was not a jukebox, and I got sick when the others danced and pumped to the soundtrack I provided.

Among other things I had let my hair grow long, like the Beatles, and people began busting my balls. One day, I decided not to sing anymore; it was time wasted. I wasn't a singer, so it was easy for me to stop, and I challenged myself to do something else. Now I sang only in the shop, changing the words of the texts at my discretion, and it attracted me. So I took it into my head that I could be the lyricist. I wrote only banality; I was not educated enough, the words were poor and the verses did not come to me. It brought me discouragement and melancholy, and after thinking it over, I stayed in the shop to refine my profession as a carpenter, hoping that in the future a great carpenter would hire me.

One day I was near the bench where I used to glue large windows outside the shop, and while I was working, a Vespa, driven by Ugo, carrying a girl in a miniskirt, braked in front of me, and Ugo told me: "Feast your eyes and fuck off, dick-head," and drove off laughing. I didn't care about him, so I paid no attention to his provocation nor the others that I would be subjected to later on. He passed the shop when he turned around, always accompanied by a girl on the back of his Vespa. A little later, he started driving a Lancia HF sports car, and inside was a girl, different from the previous ones. I thought that at this point he had dumped Sisina. Ugo seemed to no longer be working. He spent his time playing pinball in the bars and squealing around with his sports car and the car radio at full blast. He often roared around the village with his friends singing loud songs and showing off his trophies as a flag at the top of the antenna; the panties of his conquests.

Not wanting to relate to him, I began questioning myself. While I was working, I never had money in my pocket. He, instead, was fucking around, showing off rolls of bills. I heard rumors among the people that Ugo had found Eldorado, but then I figured out the real source of his money—he was fucking the girls he had in his car. He'd turned off the radio with the excuse that the music bothered him. His radio had a tape player that could record what they said through a microphone he had attached to the dashboard. All this ended up on audio cassettes in the hidden recorder. Ugo blackmailed the unfortunate girls who were forced to pay him a requested sum. With this profitable source, his greed grew so huge that he hit on as many girls as possible, until one morning he was found dead in a country lane from which he entered a piazza where there was a cistern. He lay stuck with his eyes popping out of his head and his tongue hanging out of his open mouth; a short distance away, his severed cock had been thrown on the grass. Rumor had it that he was blackmailing wives and daughters of important people, and, worse still, he had abused a mentally disabled child. The newspapers talked about it for a few days, but the investigations led to nothing, and that story was soon forgotten by everyone.

One day Andrea, at about four in the afternoon, entrusted me with a job at Teresa's house. In preparing the toolbox, he sealed a letter envelope and marked with an "X," and giving it to me told me what I had to say to Teresa.

I rang the bell, and Teresa opened the door, inviting me up; finding the entrance already open, I entered asking for permission.

"Come, Sebastiano," she told me, and just afterwards she asked me, "How old are you? You have become a handsome young man."

Somewhat embarrassed, I replied: "In a few months I'll be seventeen."

She was dressed in a gray suit, as if she were going out of her house, well combed and without her make-up. I gave her the envelope, telling her that the master would be going to the barber that evening, and then, with his family, was heading for the procession of San Francesco. Teresa opened the envelope, took out the note and read the contents. I repaired the blind by replacing the old pulley with a new one and changing the worn-out belt. After this, I went to the bathroom where I fixed the window above the bathtub. Afterwards she made me sit in the kitchen offering me a fresh glass of orzata.

The envelope contained not only a piece of paper, but also some money. She counted out five one-thousand Lira notes.

"Fuck!" I said to myself. This sum is the equivalent of my monthly salary. In the meantime, she handed me ten thousand lire, but I refused them. She dropped the bills on the table and left the kitchen with the envelope and the other money and said: "I'm going to put this away. Meanwhile, if you want, you can have something to drink," and she left. As I drank, I looked around at the gas stove, the refrigerator, and a cupboard with a turntable and forty-fives in their covers. Intrigued, I looked closer and realized that they contained records by Neil Sedaka,

Adamo, Modugno, Peppino di Capri; one in particular that seemed to be used recently attracted my attention. It was the *I Giganti* album, with the song "Tema."

Teresa in the meantime returned, and noticing me with the record in my hands told me:

"Many are old; what you have in your hands is the most recent, and if you want you can also listen while I do other things that I have to do." So saying, she left the kitchen and went into another room.

I knew that song because it was one I used to sing, and I was pleased to hear the original that was on the turntable. I was interrupted by Teresa's voice, who insistently called me to come to her. Following her voice, I reached the door of her bedroom and hesitantly crossed the threshold, seeing the quilt open as if it were a notebook; there she stood, pulling down her skirt. She looked at me sweetly, inviting me to be closer to her, and I did so, with some embarrassment, since such a thing had never happened to me.

Pulling me toward her, she rubbed her hand on the fly of my jeans and excited me, kissed me on the neck and I did the same, then she put her tongue in my mouth, and I returned it with what I was: clumsy and erect. She understood me. She pulled off her skirt and stood there in panties and bra. Now instinct overcame inhibition and taboos. I undid her bra, stroked her tits, and sucked her nipples until she was completely naked. I opened my eyes; it was the first time I saw a pussy so close, a wonder in hair. She let me caress her while she was panting with pleasure, and kneeling down she unbuttoned my trousers, and her warm hands caught my erect cock. She chiseled it with her tongue, and pecked the tip and pulled back the foreskin back to enjoy it with her eyes; her mouth closed to keep it inside; she opened it to push it out and lick it again and again.

She sat on the bed, and holding my hands in hers, she moved onto her back, raising her legs and opening her thighs, and while I saw her pussy wonderfully open, I drove my cock and stuck it inside. I was in seventh heaven. She kept raising her legs more by twisting them into my hips. I was out of control, and despite her grip, I hammered her, while she punched my kidneys so that I could move deeper inside until I ejaculated!

She held me close to her for a while, and then she told me: "Go to the bathroom, wash and dry, everything you need is there." I went back to the room and sat on the bed. Meanwhile she held a small towel under her, got up and went to the bathroom. Waiting for her, at the bedside, I noticed the picture representing the holy family hanging on the wall, and on two bedside tables of the small lampshades, the little black book of the mass and a copy of *Smiles and Songs*. Leaning on the marble top of the dresser, in front of the mirror, there was a statue of Saint Anthony in a glass bell. Next to it, there was a framed photo of Teresa's late husband, and in the middle, a small, lit oil lamp. On the console table with a mirror towered a close-up photo of Teresa as a young woman.

"I was eighteen," I heard Teresa say as I studied the details. She had just returned to the room. Then, continuing to talk, she said: "I married at nineteen, and when I was twenty-three, I was widowed; my husband Antonio died in a sanatorium. Now I am thirty-two and I live with a small pension from Antonio and with what Andrea hands me from time to time."

"I feel it ..."

"I know," she added, "in the village I'm on everyone's lips, but I don't give a damn, so, hypocritical as they are, none of them will say anything to my face."

I listened; I didn't know what to answer, and my slightly lost look settled on the drawer of the dresser where I inadvertently saw what it contained. She asked me if I was engaged, and I said no. I told her of my difficulties with the girls. She calmed me and told me: "You will find one when you least expect it. With her you play all the games that love allows, except fucking which you can do only after the marriage. I only gave myself to Antonio on our wedding night.

The next day, my mother-in-law wanted to display the sheet with my blood, as a sign of my virginity lost that night, and that I had faith in the traditions. We wanted children, but they did not come, and after several specialist visits, we had the answer: primitive sterility. Don't worry, your seed won't make me pregnant."

She had read my mind! She still wanted to talk and told me, "The girlfriend who gives in to your requests, will yield to those of other men, as the song says on the turntable. When you want, go to prostitutes, but not with those from the street; they are dirty and you can get syphilis. Instead, go to those who work at home; they might cost more, but at least they are clean. Then, if you like, come to me too, but in doing so, pay attention to how you move. The country is full of nosey people, be careful and try to warn me first."

Well, I thought, but she, reading my face, added, "Andrea is sixty-two, his wife knows he comes to me, but pretends not to know. Do you want to hear what he wrote to me on the note you brought me? Listen: 'Dear Love, Sunday morning, before going hunting, I will pass by you.' That asshole! Only his shotgun works. He can't stay hard, and soon it will only serve to pee."

We went back into the kitchen together, and the record player spun with the arm and the needle in the last groove. She lifted the disk from the record player and put it in the case, then took one from Neil Sedaka, set it down on the turntable, and moving the arm, she lowered the needle onto the disk. Neil sang "What Have They Done to the Moon," one of Teresa's favorite songs from her youth, and while she was still offering me a brace with her back to me, I took the money and put it in the middle of the record stack. We said goodbye between kisses, and finally she said to me: "It was nice!"

I went downstairs, thinking of her mouth and her vagina that had been drinking my virginity. I was the number four on her list, where the husband was the first, Andrea the second, and the third was in the drawer of the dresser: a vibrator with which Teresa used to ease the loneliness of the night and the boredom of the day. Usually the whores are called beautiful at night. Teresa was not a whore, and for me she was simply beautiful by day.

After I returned to the shop the next day, Master Andrea told me: "I was told that it took you a long time to do what I ordered you." I figured he'd ask that question from the way he greeted me when I walked in. I replied, softly: "The pulley, although it was new, had some flaws, and took a long time to replace. Not only that, but in replacing the hinges of the window to bathtub, it didn't close well; it needed to be planed and since I didn't have one, I gave up and promised to return when you thought it would be appropriate."

Master Andrea seemed to swallow the story, but from that day on he showed mistrust towards me. I already had my cock on my mind. I could not even think of his headaches and doubts about me, as they fed his usual spasms of gossiping about everything.

I reflected on my failures with the girls, the music, the words, the club and the band: all holes in water! I was learning a trade, but my income was low because I was underpaid. All this worried me while new things happened around me, like the schools that the students had occupied in May. There were also the first protest marches in June, making headlines in all the newspapers about the hippies who praised love and condemned war. The word *Vietnam* was on everyone's lips, and the police charged the protesters using tear gas, who responded by throwing Molotov cocktails. It was a battle between poor humans; the sons of workers against other so-called privileged sons who were studying. Through all this I felt like a fish out of water there, in the shop, talking to the wood and musing on my mental elaborations.I feigned ingorance over what was happening to him, and then I swore to myself that I would do my best to feed myself.

I began to buy books, but I did not fully understand them. At the same time, I sought new friendships, and over time I was disappointed. Nothing worked out and I was on the verge of paranoia. For spite, one evening, with some older guys, I went to see the prostitutes.

The first thing I saw was a lit red-light bulb that hung on an olive tree near a gate that stayed open. We parked on the side of the main road, and entered on foot, as the square was full of cars. Between the beds, many people were pissing, and then talking to each other using vulgar language interspersed with profanities.

I was excited because my buddies had thrown a porn magazine in my face. The pimp made us sit in a living room full of guys. There were just three whores. Each fuck cost two thousand lire for an average time of about a quarter of an hour. My turn came. The whore was kind in her way, and cold in deed. I touched her body; it was freezing, and I could not get excited. She washed my cock, before licking it artfully, but I was still limp. I masturbated, and finally in erection, ejaculated in her hands as soon as she put on the condom. There was no passion in her body, and mine was filled with disgust and doubt. I dressed, while she said: "Don't take it so hard, it always happens like that the first time."

A few days later, like a script, my story of the whores went around the country. It all started with one of those empty heads with his mouth full of words who got thrown out of the place, so he told the story while getting his hair cut. Barbers, you know, never cut hair or shave in silence. Customers who followed each other always referred to the hearsay, and the news ran unrestrained throughout the country. Master Andrea threatened to tell my father, who in turn had already learned from others. In fact, my father told me: "Look for a girlfriend. Don't go back to whores anymore and open your eyes for one you'll get engaged to."

Speaking to the bookseller, I confided my difficulties in reading the books I bought from him. He answered me with a phrase from a writer: "Reading requires education, and haste is not part of the game."

I understood the meaning of this maxim, and I started again to read. In the evening, in bed, before going to sleep, I read about fifteen pages, other nights more than twenty, and so I no longer belonged to any party, nor did I take interest in what was happening around me. That voluntary exile lasted several months and was especially pleasing in the fruits I was beginning to pick. The more fruits I gathered, the more I learned to know myself. I was educating myself, but I was still fragile in character. More time passed, and my daily life was divided between home, work, and reading, until in my neighborhood a family came to live with a fifteen-year-old daughter. She was Sara, and the attraction between us was mutual and like lightning. I courted her with pride and she was enthusiastic about it, so much so that she said yes, and I got excited. Her younger brother found out about us because he was spying for his parents, forcing me to come to terms with them. They accepted me willingly and allowed me to accompany her to the knitwear store where she was employed and pick her up after work, weather and conditions permitting.

One day I hummed a song on the street that led to her work. Sara was absorbed in her thoughts but listened to me. Suddenly she told me: "Now I remember, it was you who sang with the Eta Beta. I heard you at my cousin's party a few years ago, when you had long hair and sang 'The Woman of My Friend,' which I loved. I didn't recognize you with short hair. Why did you leave the group?" I told her the truth, and she answered: "You could have become rich and famous." I replied, "Meeting you, I found my treasure." She welcomed my appreciation with happiness in her eyes, and we kissed with tenderness.

Just a month had passed and already we began to discover sex. We were in a hurry and soon she allowed me to go beyond kisses. One afternoon we marched to work, and taking the side roads on to the route designated by her parents, we took a path that led to the hollow where she had lived before she moved. There were some furnishings left, and her father had not yet handed the keys to the owner. There were four rooms. Sara had approached the stone table outside on the square, and knowing where to look, found the big key with which she opened the front door. On our feet, we began to kiss each other until we entered. It was dark, and enough light came through the windows for what we were about to do. We both gasped, and the atmosphere excited us more. I kissed her neck and her tits. I put my hands in her panties, titillating her clit, until we both sank into intense pleasure. We stopped only for a few moments, and our agonized breaths ended in the open door of reason, and I said to her, "Should we continue?"

She winked at me, consenting. We began to kiss again, and the tenderness took on an air of mystery even though we were both still excited. I touched her between her thighs, pulled her panties off and rubbed her clit again. She in the meantime took off her clothes and bra, and I took off my pants and T-shirt, and pulled my dick out of my underpants while she bent down and grabbed it in her hands. With greedy eyes she opened her mouth and swallowed it for a moment. Then she would push it back, wrapping it with her tongue until, sitting on the bench, with legs up and heels pressing the hem, she opened her thighs. Clinging to her knees to stay in balance, she showed me the lips of her vagina that I was about to kiss, dilating so that my tongue could play inside. I was lost blissfully in the Eden protected by her black bush, and with my cock in my hands I was looking for the way in, but she held my wrist, and said to me:

"Stop. I don't want to do this."

I obeyed her, though I did not want to, and letting go of my wrist, she took my cock and brought it closer to her vagina as soon as the glans slid all around, only to pull it inside just enough not to affect her virginity. Enjoying this she put my dick back in her mouth, and the game continued until I came between her tits. In the pause followed, I reflected on why I had not insisted on penetrating her. Her refusal had been enough, but was it also the dogmas of the Church that raised the head of sin: Do not commit impure acts, do not fornicate—that meant not to fuck and not masturbate; the seed you lose is an unborn child. Crushed by these fears, I felt defeat, naive as Candide and gullible. Sara, on the other hand, showed that she was a very precocious scoundrel in doing what she wanted, and in keeping others from doing what she did not want to do. The game, therefore, was led by her.

There was still some time at our disposal, and after eating all the chocolate bars, we went back at it, on a mattress pulled out of the back of the bench case. She got on all fours with her head on my thighs and I under her, and clinging to her buttocks I stuck her face between her thighs and licked her pussy. With Sara on the other side, I masturbated working in her mouth and tongue, and it seemed a fiery crater that instead of erupting swallowed, bringing my adrenaline and passion to the fullest. My sperm ended up in that crater while her cunt spread a liquid nectar that settled on my tongue and wet my mouth. We left ourselves exhausted, and after having put on our clothes we put the mattress back and went out.

It was already twilight. Hand in hand and without realizing it, we returned to the village. Along the way she told me, satisfying my curiosity, that in the locker room of her company, among the girls, they shared porn magazines, and that their weaning from their parents' morality had begun. At six in the evening, I accompanied Sara home, pretending to have left from her work. After that I returned to my room where I remembered Teresa's words: "Do everything that erotic games allow you to do, but do not deflower her if it's not your wedding night."

Sara also lived, perhaps, with the blinders that those of the Church passed to her. I was mortified, and I thought of marrying her as soon as possible. Her brother, like all the spies, was also in the pay of his sister, and through bribes he allowed us to lock ourselves in their room, while he remained upstairs to think about how to invest the pay of Judas. Sara opened her mobile bed, the other belonged to Judas, and soon we played with sex, turning around, doing what was called sixty-nine.

At the end of the scheduled time I accompanied her to the knitwear factory, stopping first at the bar, where I bought cigarettes and she always had an ice cream with her favorite flavor: chocolate and cream.

Sara's parents both worked, her mother in a fruit and vegetable store, and her father in the building industry. For them, work began at seven in the morning and ended at three in the afternoon. We insisted on asking them to go out on our own, at least on holidays. They accepted, but provided that Judas stayed with us. We understood the reason later. Sara and I bought the silence that Alfonso Giuda then sold to her mother. To undo the knot, we promised them that we would be married soon. There was the meeting of the two families to discuss Sara's trousseau. We would marry after my military service, and before then, we couldn't be alone without the presence of her brother, except when I walked with her to work.

Along the road that bordered the company's building, the youngsters stopped in their cars listening to music, while waiting for the workers to come out. The cars were modern, from the Mini Mino, the Giulietta, to the convertible Spider, and they bought them thanks to the miracle of Santa Cambiale. In addition to displaying fashionable clothes and handbags, the workers became photoromaniacs that they had unconsciously swallowed in the vortex of the identification process. Those photographic scenes of beautiful and rich couples who lived stories written especially for those magazines, were fucking the brains of those who bought them and read, and for those who received them on loan with subliminal messages to follow the fashion! The publishing houses had planned everything and thought only of selling goods. Whoever paid money for the purchase did it out of narcissism by paying cash for those stories in episodes, happy and unconscious to be the penniless that fed on those dreams. Sara was not far behind, and in a short time she let herself be seduced by that false well-being, wishing for the myths she was exposed to. She, on the other hand, was engaged to a former singer who was a carpenter.

My military service kept us distant. I wrote to her often, but she, who was not familiar with the pen, wrote me only two postcards. I took leave and went back to work; the goal I had set for myself was to make as much money as possible to be able to marry Sara. For this reason, I used to work overtime and take on my own work that Master Andrea would allow me to do in his own workshop, obviously after working hours. With Sara, we consumed the sexual meal with the leftovers of my time, and we got into it with petting. We would have the complete meal, by her will, on our wedding night. Time flowed fast, and between caresses and kisses, I realized that her yearning was dying, that everything was getting cold, and her passion was fading. I asked her why, and while her sentences were honest, they kicked me in the face. She told me she had fallen in love with someone else, and she did not know how to tell me. In the face of evidence, I collapsed.

Respecting her decision, which of course I did not share, I broke off the engagement, even though she had been the one to tear our love story apart. I came back with my tail between my legs and the umpteenth pain of my daily life. I went to work, but with less effort than in the recent past, and I decided to get my driver's license; I only needed the practice exam. That's when I stopped reading my books. After two months I tried to emerge from the quagmire in which Sara had pushed me. I was about to succeed, but she sent me a message through her brother telling me that she wanted to talk to me. I said yes and met her with some hesitation. I listened to her justifications and ended up deciding that I had to give her a chance. She had recognized that she had made a mistake, that the guy she had fallen in love with was in fact only a mistake, and that I remained her man. In short, I agreed to mend our relationship.

In the period that followed, I had returned to being her official fiancé who accompanied her to work, receiving in exchange the incomplete meal during sexual games while on the false road of that relationship, Sara was plotting something. She told me one evening, and I crumbled. The next day I went to the shop and he fired me. I put my stuff in my suitcase, and I went out of my house to review the places that, in exchange for a few moments of happiness, now crushed me with so much sadness.

Come evening, I got on the train. Alone in the compartment, I looked out the window and saw only the darkness. I thought about Sara's last words: "I was forced to get back with you. Otherwise, my parents would have kept me in the house. You were my ticket out. We can get married if you want, but I cannot guarantee you anything. You're a good boy and you do not deserve this, but try to understand me. I want to live."

She forgot to add: great! She had become greedy, and I was just a carpenter who lived day to day. I remembered the first record I had given her, *Concert of the Alumni del Sole*, and the last song heard at the jukebox in the station bar, "I Giardini di Marzo," by Lucio Battisti.

What an actress Sara had become!

I threw the memories out of the window with the tears of the last cry. In the city I looked for a place to live and a job. I was lucky, because an antique furniture restorer was looking for a carpenter. After a trial week, he hired me. Everything seemed resolved, but Sara's memory was hard to lose. I beat solitude by going to the prostitutes. I knew the area where they lured their customers, and with them I negotiated the price, time after time, and then went to a hotel they trusted. I did not fuck them because of the first and last experience of a few years before. They sucked my cock, giving professional blowjobs, and each with her own technique. For them, this was an art. They faked orgasms that made me neither hot nor cold. For me it was just important that I had stuck my dick in their mouths to squirt my seed in their throats as agreed. Therefore, they knew that with my seed they swallowed my anger, and I did not care about their fake orgasms. The bitterness, however, persisted, and we kept at it until late autumn.

In the first days of winter, I returned to my hometown. At home, they welcomed me benevolently; there was the Christmas tree. I decided to take a walk, but my mother warned me and said: "Be careful, it snowed tonight, cover yourself well."

The village was all whitewashed, and the narrow and twisted alleyways I took led to where a gentleman faced away from me, painting a canvas on a trestle. I knew that man, and he came to town every year to paint the neighborhoods and landscapes of our countryside, but only in the summer. Seeing him that day on that whitewashed square surprised me. Observing his work, without bothering him, I noticed that he removed the canvas from the easel and placed it on the ground with its surface in the air, and the frame on the snow. Then he lit a cigar and took a few puffs. Turning around himself he realized that I was watching him. It was Vittorio Viviani.

I greeted him, and he motioned for me to come closer. I introduced myself, and as if nothing had happened, he asked me my opinion on his painting. I, without false modesty, told him that I was not the right person to judge his painting, and I mentioned my attempts to paint when I was a teenager. I was expecting the usual, somewhat surly answer; he not only encouraged me, but told me: "Why don't you try again? You'll be wrong with the first one, but who knows how many other paintings you'll try and if you keep at it, passion for creating works will blossom, and you'll be enveloped by that drug made of canvas, brushes and colors."

He had managed to convince me. I also told him about my attempts at writing, but he silenced me and then said: "Choose one thing, write or paint." Thanking him I bade him a warm goodbye; as I walked away, Vittorio took the canvas off the ground, put it on the easel, and resumed painting the little square with the fountain in the middle. Walking in the snow I wondered if Vittorio would go to the cemetery, as he did every year; his friend Sergio Nicolò De Bellis died in the late 1940s, after a lifetime dedicated to the art of painting. His works were denigrated and then banned by the Fascist regime in all the exhibitions because they were considered communist. He had died of a heart attack, at least this was the official version. They found him dead in the room of his home near the Brera Academy. He lived as a poor man, and never hid behind false identities.

I went back home, and no one talked about my latest events. My brother was sixteen, and my sisters were thirteen and twelve. In the house as usual, my father had built the Nativity creche. With the paper from cement bags he had created the mountains, covering them with moss, while the huts had been built with empty boxes of detergent, which he then had colored. In a corner behind the table he brought out the ivy tied with string to a strip of wood, and from its branches hung taralli, pomegranates, oranges, and some mandarins. At the moment when everything was ready, we added the clay statues depicting the Madonna, St. Joseph, and the Child Jesus with all the shepherds and other characters of the time.

After the holidays, I went on my way, leaving them the phone number for my new shop, and resumed everyday life: work, home, and endless reading to discover new authors. From the window I admired the surrounding terraces with television antennas that increased visibly. Everyone was now used to seeing and listening to that whore of television that now dominated almost every home, teaching consumption of all that it offered.

I returned to the canvas, brushes, and colors and started painting again. It was a long time before I had any decent results, but I never gave up, and the desire to paint gripped me in its jaws.

One day the boss called me to tell me that they wanted me on the phone. I picked up the phone and answered. It was my brother who told me some bad news from the country. Master Andrea had died between Teresa's thighs, and she had gone out of her mind. The same day she threw herself down from the balcony, killing herself. They had no funeral, because of all the gossip of the bigoted of our town.

The other news was about Tonietta. She had her brothers arrested because they had raped her on alternate evenings, and they had also made her pregnant. Perhaps they believed that with the act of violating the flesh of their sister, the legacy remained in the family, and so Tonietta also ran the risk of going crazy.

Mortified, I put the receiver in its place, and went back to work with a darkened mood, as if I needed some brightness. I did not smoke cigarettes, but I smoked pot on a Sunday morning by accident, while I placed the easel on a rock that allowed me to paint the sea. Sitting in a circle, around an almost extinguished fire, a group of boys were singing and playing the guitar, between songs they pulled out a joint. They saw me and to invited me to join them. I willingly accepted, and joined the group. I soon learned to smoke it with skill, and I already knew how to get it, and where to get it. I began to go to concerts, and while working I recalled years and years of memories that had walked in a mental territory closed between four bones, precisely my skull box.

Memories beautiful and ugly ran free as nomads, and finally in order of time the image of Maria Clara. Beyond a few days, the Nomads would bring their songs of love, protest, and freedom into the theater.

In an agreement with the shop owner, I worked overtime for the whole week. This allowed me to be free on Saturday afternoons to go to the concert. At the end of the working day, after having lunch in a restaurant, I set out for the train. While I waited, I began to look at the poster that portrayed Guccini and the Nomads together; there was a lot of time before the concert started, but I took the next train. On the train I sat down easily; it was half empty. I got off at a stop in the square in front of the Odeon theater. The newspaper stand was nearby where I had agreed to meet with Maria Clara. A month had passed since I had met her, and we hadn't seen each other since then.

Now the days were longer, full of light, and the weather was milder and warmer. I sat down on a bench hoping that time passed quickly, and started fighting old preoccupations. Who was I? Walking alone, who had I become? I was, or at least I felt I was, an illegitimate son of that era, and out of place, when the bands performed at Monterey, Woodstock, the Isle of Wight, and New York for the Concert for Bangladesh. I was the illegitimate son and half-brother of that generation that was called by different names like *beat, hippies,* and *free generation.* Right then I stopped singing and cut my hair, but could not pass as a nice guy.

Unconsciously I had been bogged down in the humus of provincialism. In this area I was not at ease, paying for the abandonment of those events that happened on an international scale, and getting kicked in the balls by all the pretenders, the hypocrites, and the cynics, Sara included. All these were sons and brothers of Papa Carosello, a popular product offered by television, which like a mistress, pockets the cash. In return, it transmitted black-and-white images of dancers, old films and drama, a single newscast, and sheep that grazed grass on the fields around the time of Paestum. In the cinemas, however, concerts were projected based on successful songs and interpreted by the singers themselves. These half-brothers belonged fully to the middle-class bourgeois, children of the nouveau riche. For me they were dwarfs massaged in mediocrity, and in that guise, they seemed like giants who were fringed by that new God—money. I received offenses and epithets from these dwarfs, and yet I never bowed to them, only to the books I read. Later in the cinemas I saw all the live concerts now become normal movies. Suspending my thoughts, I looked around, but Maria Clara hadn't arrived. So, I got up and headed for the box office, where I bought the entrance tickets and went back to the kiosk hoping that Maria Clara would arrive in time. Among the books displayed by the newsagent I chose one, and I bought it; while leafing through it, I caught Maria Clara, who came toward me with an agitated gesture. After saying hello, I asked, "Are you worried about the exams? I see you're a little agitated."

"I'm upset, but not for the exams; they won't happen for a while," she replied calmly, and added: "Your friends, those of the Renault R4, tried to approach me by offering me a concert ticket. When I refused one of them struck me violently, and I managed to escape from his clutches I do not even know how. "

She, poor thing, did not know that that night, after our first meeting, I had a fight with them. I told her of the events that occurred and the reasons for my dispute with them, and she said that she understood, replying, "I flipped when they attacked, forcing me to accept the ticket; after I threw it back in their faces, they fled, almost crashing the car."

After calming down, she noted the book I was holding and asked, "What are you reading?"

"It's by an American author, *Spoon River Anthology.*"

"I already read it; I'm sure you'll like it."

We walked towards the theater, joining the others who meanwhile began, with great difficulty, to smoke one joint after another. We joined them; after all, we were all born after the Second World War—a generation full of illusions for the future, probably conceived by couples wooed by vintage films like *Chains, Torment,* and actresses like Clara Calamai for the first time bare-breasted under the watchful eye of a camera. This generation was the living product of the songs heard on the radio, or a gramophone subject to frequent changes of needle to not damage the discs. She was dancing, and she did it under the close supervision of relatives. Some of the children of this generation were the fruits of couples fleeing their parents, resulting in a marriage celebrated at 5:00 am in a sacristy, to repair the shame and rebuild a relationship with God. Those who had answers to this generation were always reticent, with true or false modesty.

At this point I wondered if the next generation would have posed the same questions about the songs and the images that seduced my generation, that gave them birth. They will want to know about the Prague Spring, about who immolated himself in protest, and my generation will tell them that it had all been an illusion and we were disappointed. Above all we were impotent, in the face of massacres in our own homes, and where the only real aspect that everyone knew concerned the number of dead. Often those who went to jail had been branded and slammed on the front page by the secret services in the pay of the puppets who in turn protected the true culprits, avoiding giving them what they deserved. These puppets were subjected to trials, but thanks to the tongues of their lawyers and by means of bribes, they evaded justice, and when conviction for some was certain, they managed to escape from prison, and who knows how? The homeland jails, however, were full of chicken thieves.

My generation, if it will survive without suffering too many losses for premature senility and dementia, will have to find the courage to speak with honesty denouncing the dishonesty of those people called Pinocchio, an infamous and transformist race.

The Nomads and Francesco Guccini were greeted with a long applause. We, full of adrenaline, were ready to add our voices to their songs.

Augustus and Francis sang together "God is Dead," and even if apparently without following any order, the songs alternated without any pause. As a finale, Augustus and Francis sang "Auschwitz," a song that saddened us, because it narrated the greatest planned massacre in the name of one race to the detriment of another. "Io Vagabondo" followed with the final song: "Up there I was God," and God was resurrected, but remained in heaven continuing to be invoked. Piccola Storia Ignobile made us understand how with money, and for money, you could abort a fetus. He made us understand that, for a while he was carrying him on his lap, he did not evaluate the extent of that drama that occurred during a road accident. Francesco ended his part by finishing with "Poisoned," an invective against the social schemes that left us flattened and beggars, inculcating the official culture that dominated us by force. "Poisoned" was a cry against those who beat us down.

The Nomads and Guccini left with our applause. We, with goosebumps on our skin, tears in our eyes and the lumps in our throats, left the theater, thinking that the universal key of music and words was the passport for our consciences and for those of future generations. Walking in the square we tried to rearrange the ideas and restart the speeches of the previous month going back to the other concert. We realized that we were living by the arguments of philosophers, poets and pacifists, or revolutionaries, anarchy and so on. I had learned these subjects before from books with some reservations that happened because I did not live them. Now it was all different. Maria Clara had lived other stories and now she was addressing these issues from her point of view. She was cultured and instinctive, and education made her confident in her choices. She was sniffing out those in whom to put her trust; I had the impression that she was a psychic. Both pinned by the events, trust was mutual, and this was what made us meet, discover, and be attracted to the sound of a violin.

Later, we went to the pizzeria, and for a while we did nothing but recycle the speeches made up to then. She told me that she wrote poetry, and I told her that sometimes I tried, even if I always ended up burning everything. She spoke of herself in a very humble and sincere language, telling me of her sad childhood like mine, and of the adverse fate in those times for those who had been born a woman. She hoped to understand people, even if others did not give them credit for what she said and wrote. Unlike me, she did not burn anything; on the contrary, she continued to write with greater awareness. I, in turn, told her about myself, about my past, and about the uncertainty of the future. I spoke to her of the paintings I painted, of my desire to realize myself. Much was the poverty, however, that made up the great mosaic of doubts that darkened the street and the blind alleys that I traveled on.

On Sunday morning we went to the beach. The small boats swayed on the shallow water of the harbor, and we walked along the shore trying to draw conclusions from our talk. We spent most of the day walking non-stop, almost getting sunstroke. The truth, however, was another, we walked without a destination, between beaches and weeds that surrounded the land. We were connected. Getting to know each other closely involved a bit of shyness and tension, unconsciously, which always meandered between the two of us.

Night came and Maria Clara had to go home. After accompanying her, I walked all alone through the deserted streets, where my memories began to assail me. I found it curious that when I was not in the company of someone, memories came into my mind that took over everything else. I was walking in a daze under a pitch-black sky that threatened rain, almost without realizing where I was going. I was there, on a sidewalk, and tried in vain to steal thoughts of what happened that night, so as not to suffer loneliness. The light from the street lamps fell dull on the tiles that paved the sidewalk. What a night, I thought, not a single star to keep me company, while an icy wind did not spare even a millimeter of my skin. My gaze pierced the road to lean where a light glow illuminated a figure of a woman with her hands outstretched warming over a fire; she wore a very short skirt and a knitted shawl on her shoulders adorning her body.

"Hey," she shouted to me as soon as I was there.

"Hey," she kept shouting at me. I pretended not to hear her, and she yelled louder.

"Hey, you want to fuck? Come on, nice boy. It costs little to fuck me."

"No," I answered dryly.

After a grimace of disapproval, she fell silent. It was not a question of money. I had stopped going to whores; I no longer wanted to know the mechanical love transmitted by that cold meat that opened only for money; I was looking for something else. I walked and immersed in these reflections I soon arrived at the railway station without realizing it and entered. I had always hated the stations. They gave me a sense of sadness. There were always people leaving and people coming, and people crying. There was hardly anyone left, I immediately decided to leave the scene of this daily theater that never compensated its actors. Once out of the station I headed for some public gardens located a little further up. Zigzagging among the flowerbeds, I gave myself a break, sitting on the edges that bounded them, in order to catch the smells of the flowers that, alas, did not reach my nostrils because the cold of the night froze each petal. Maria Clara, instead, entered it like a delicious scent, until it reached the depths of my thoughts. I thought and thought back to our first and mysterious meeting at the concert, to many other little things that, added together, solidified this relationship of friendship, or perhaps, of love just blossomed!

It was all clear to me now, I had fallen in love with her from the beginning, even though it was equally clear that there were a few years between us. These beautiful thoughts were interrupted by the sharp siren of an ambulance, which in addition to shattering my concentration, broke the silence that surrounded me.

At this point, with a glance, I began to follow the trajectory of the headlights. Who could be the unfortunate traveler, who had unconsciously paid his ticket, perhaps, for his last trip? By now I also lost interest in this. Depression was everywhere, and when I got to the neighborhood where I lived, I sat down on the sidewalk to rest. In the meantime, I sent the third degree of judgment against my thoughts, getting up suddenly to open the door of the house and climb the stairs. The house where I lived, in fact, was the last floor of an old building, the attic of the building where I painted. While my choices were maturing, they never landed on anything and doubts multiplied, confusing the present and making the future increasingly uncertain. How many seasons had passed, and I had not been aware of the weather. Consciousness of that miserable way of living alone had also made me a lost man.

I was going backwards, towards what was my childhood, when my father took me on the bicycle, making me sit on the bar, and I for fear of losing my balance, clung to the handlebars trying not to fall. On October 4th, a good number of years ago, my father quit work early to take the family to the convent that was on the hill, where the friars who occupied it celebrated the feast of Saint Francis. He made us wash and dress up for my mother's party, and together we went. My mother pushed the bicycle that had a luggage rack on which sat my sisters, while the handlebars were steered by my father, and my brother and I were next to him walking on foot. On the way he stopped at an oven and bought some focaccia, and from a stall among the many not far away, he took some olives from the lime barrel. Tired from the steep climb that we faced, we arrived at the convent, and exhausted, but happy, we prepared to enter the church to hear Holy Mass. At the end, we sat down on a landing with another three steps, where at the top there was a large cross that rose in the dark, and under a sky illuminated by the party lights, we finally ate focaccia and olives.

"How much time has passed since then! How long have I been sitting at your table! Dear father, your son is an anarchist. For him, there is nothing that matters more than freedom."

I was tired of going around with blinders, fed up with suffering, swallowing and suffering. My balls were busted by the moralism of others, which aimed only to make me bow my head and always say yes, yes.

"For these reasons, dear father, now I am here alone, just like a dog, to masturbate my mind trying to find an inner balance."

My childhood, if it had the roots of a disaster, was not my father's fault. Later, if my crises poisoned adolescence in progress, I blamed it on my people's provincialism. At the age of twenty, I was exasperated; I owed it to false friends and to those who laughed behind my back, making me feel that I was worthless, unable to offer tenderness. Actually, I was just an unlucky boy. With Sara, I put aside anticonformism, and I was integrating into the system. I was putting my "head right," as was usually said, but my poverty was caught unaware by the false wealth that others showed off. The relationship with Sara was not love, because she was fooled by appearances, such as luxury cars and money. Dear father, since then the desire to leave the country was born, to breathe with my lungs, to finally reason with my head.

"Dear father, I am still still looking for myself. For the first time in my life I feel free, even though I have remained a poor man. I met Maria Clara, a beautiful woman in her simplicity. You see, dear father, me and simplicity, we always got along."

With my mind turned to memories, I was agitated, trying hard to fall asleep, without succeeding. I stared at the thoughts of her, now the dominant figure of my visions, and in the meantime, I smoked a joint. Dreams and visions overlapped, subtracting from the will the possibility of meddling in that mystical prefabricated reality. I was flying at dizzying heights. I flew up to the gates of the beyond, where a voice that came muffled to my ears whispered to me:

"There is no place for your imagination here." Then I walked over a rainbow, like a marionette. Dreams hurried by, they grabbed me and tossed me between one color and another of the rainbow. I was alone, completely naked, and if it rains? In dreams one becomes a fool. It cannot rain on rainbows. I convinced myself that I was safe at that height.

I woke up with a start, ran to turn the water tap, I was very thirsty, and I drank a little in large gulps. After that, I went out onto the little terrace, and watched what was about to happen. The dawn was resting on the roofs and the last shadows of the night slid down along the walls. Here's the new day, I said to myself, it's all here, with the same problems as yesterday. I went back in and hopped back to bed hoping to go back to sleep. I still needed dreams, and I closed my eyes and wished I could take them by surprise. On the contrary, however, they were to surprise me. A face-to-face with my unconscious was born again.

Maria Clara, with her eyes wide open, was sitting in a yoga position, holding a large book on her knees, from whose pages copious tears fell in the darkness. I always knew she was afraid of the dark. I took courage, and so I got out of bed. I walked around the room, hoping for some idea to kill time, because I had to keep my mind busy. I managed to find a canvas on the easel, then dampen the necessary colors and started to work. I painted the sky of a light blue, and in the center of the canvas a seagull. When the work was finished, I had painted a seagull with wings spread out as if it wanted to escape from that sky, but it remained there, since the desire to paint had passed away. I cleaned the palette and brushes, put everything back in place, and left the house.

I headed for the port, and here I looked at the real gulls. They flew free, splashing around in the waves, and one abandoned the flock to fly farther and farther. I went home and threw myself on the bed crying. I did not paint a real one; I felt nothing I did was worth anything anymore. I was in full crisis and I knew it, but who to ask for help, if not myself? I thought of suicide as a way of escape, it was a long time that anguish had me in his lap, and I stood with him hand in hand, as if the best living conditions should fall from the sky. In this depressing state, I could not stay home.

Maria Clara had graduated and applied to the school board to teach. In the meantime, she had changed homes because the space was no longer sufficient to give lessons to the students in difficulty and prepare them for the exams. With a friend of hers, Lorenza, a teacher herself, she had found a two-room flat on a ground floor, sharing the expenses. After work, I went to visit her, but not every day, because of the commitments and the distance from her new home. Saturday evening and Sunday, however, we were always together. Hand in hand, like teenagers, we strolled through public parks, avenues, squares, and on the pier, to enjoy the horizon that divided the sea from the sky. On other occasions we went to the cinema, or we left town to go and listen to the musical groups suited to our tastes. Until then there were only kisses on the cheek between us and some hugs. We were too shy to do more!

In the evening, at dinner, I resumed telling her about my past, and she listened open-mouthed. I told her about the paintings I had made and packed in the attic, and invited her to see them. She gladly accepted. We finished dinner, and I took her back home, and she promised to see my paintings the following Sunday. On the way back, I smoked a joint. I spent the night struggling with dreams, a bit for the joint and a little for the wine I had drunk.

One of the dreams was this: It was sunset, and I was pushing a bizarre cart making a huge effort, even if it was empty. I was going down a pine-lined avenue when, suddenly, in front of me, three girls appeared, all about fifteen years old. They talked to each other using incomprehensible language, and in my presence, they began hopping around me as if they were dancing. I had no way of going beyond this road because the dream vanished. I ended up fishing for another dream that had something in common with the previous one: In one room there were my paintings hanging on the walls. On the floor, everywhere, there were many sheets written with green ink, and on some my handwriting, which I recognized at times. Maria Clara bent down to pick one up and read the contents. Then I found myself alone wandering through deserted streets, and suddenly people came out from every corner, running chaotically. My partner, on the other hand, tried to come out of a tree-lined street (the same place where I had met the three girls in the previous dream), holding some sheets in her right hand. I could not distinguish them well enough to understand if they were the same sheets of the room of the paintings, while she ran wildly dodging the people who grew more and more numerous. She noticed me, came to meet me, took me by the hand and led me through other paths and paths that existed only in dreams. I found myself walking through nothingness; she reappeared sitting quietly next to a long-haired boy who played the electric guitar and was saying or singing something. She took off her clothes, stripping herself completely. Very naturally she gave him her body. Black with rage, I grabbed her and pushed her away from him, in despair. I was looking for her lips, hoping she would kiss me, then I cried with tears of an old evil, and I cried until I woke her up. Now she was awake, now she saw me, I existed, I loved her, but I was afraid of this love, and maybe I didn't deserve it! She opened her eyes, smiled at me, took my hands in hers and in those moments of sweetness our lips met tenderly. I do not know how long we embraced; we cannot measure time in dreams.

Frankly, I loved analyzing dreams, because they were a wake-up call for something that had already happened or will happen. Dream analysis helped me understand what in reality was confused, enclosed and sealed under a form of apology to oneself.

*

On Sunday morning I went to her parents' house, and I took her to my place. Opening the front door wide, I said: "Welcome to my disorder." In my joke there was no sarcasm, because the mess really was there. She examined my paintings while being fascinated, and told me:

"All the paintings reflect your character, your mood when you painted," adding in a low voice:

"Can you take me home. I am not well. I'm feeling dirty; my period is coming."

She told me that she would come the following Sunday to continue looking at the paintings. That week flew without my realizing it, and on Sunday morning I was already there waiting for her at the door of her house. She left with a box of colored tubes in her hand, and when she was near me, she said: "Here are your colors and my pains, and I wish I could mix them with you."

Her look was sincere, and she hugged me intensely, offering me her mouth; we ended up kissing tenderly. It was the first kiss of real lovers.

"Today it ends like this," she told me, handing me the color box as a gift and adding: "Take it with you. I do not want to be by your side when you open it. Let me hear, I care."

That said, she went back to the house after saying goodbye. I was stunned by what happened; I walked away quickly and sat down on the first bench I found. I was trembling and opened the box. A whole range of oil tubes was arranged in order, and between them was a vial of linseed oil and a bottle of turpentine. There was a large notebook under the lid, held closed by a rubber band. I took it in my hands, freed it from the rubber band, and opened it. On the first page was written: "*Just for your eyes, something of me. Maria Clara.*" It was her diary, but it seemed abnormal because it did not have dates.

Today I am twenty-two years old. I have good reason to bite my past, swallow it and throw up pure ink on this diary that will see you as my first and only reader.

A white page followed, and on the other was written: *Once, like all teenagers, I entrusted my emotions to a diary. In my spare time I updated it, noting all the impressions of the day. I did not express judgments, but with myself I was ruthless, and examined my life through long reflections.*

I was fourteen and had recently graduated from middle school. I wanted to attend high school. One day the diary disappeared, and I was never able to find it again. Based on my mother's behavior, I think she took it away from me, thus emptying my fragile age of the most intimate memories. Many years have passed since then, and I have never had a diary to report on myself. Today, however, I feel the need to retrace with my mind's eye the tortuous paths that lead me back to my adolescence.

In a beautiful handwriting, on the next page, the diary continued: *My study and afternoon homework were accompanied by the sound of a piano that my neighbor across the house played with gentle skill. Riccardo was a student of my music. During those hours, he performed, interrupting that music with Beethoven's "For Elise." Every afternoon he repeated this piece almost in full, so that for me it had become the soundtrack of my reflections. Among the textbooks and written assignments that I wrote in my school notebooks, these notes were for the boyfriends I pretended to have, the hot ones for the boys I liked the most. That piano distracted me, and it put me in a mood in which I felt melancholy and enthusiasm, happiness and disappointment, all at the same time.*

My mother's greed was a bottomless pit, and while she was well off, she could not enjoy the comfort in which she lived. From the early hours of the morning she flaunted herself in the mirror, changed her hair to platinum blonde, put lipstick on her lips, and strutting, with her bag in hand, she left the house. In vain steps she wandered through the streets of the neighborhoods, a new imitation of a Marilyn Monroe. Her purpose was to go to homes to practice innoculations and home treatments. In fact, in her purse, she had a small metal box that contained a glass syringe stored in water. At work, she first instructed the patient to lie down on the bed, then placed the container on the kitchen stove, and while it was heating to a boil, she extracted the syringe, cooled it, and after inserting the plunger, placed the needle and aspirated the medicine, preparing to inject it into the patient intramuscularly.

My father was a general worker at the town hall. Without a profession, he was an assistant of all the municipal offices. Greedy for money like my mother, he lent money to third parties for usury by managing his grandmother's pension that he used to tend his traps for unfortunates. My parents were a couple of hungry people dependent on money, and wherever they invested, the interests they collected multiplied, and the capital grew visibly. To others, however, they looked like a couple of simpletons who barely reached the end of the month with what they earned. Behind their masks they plied their charms to procure new victims, and in these things they possessed an infallible flair. With her services as a nurse, my mother was also held in high esteem by the needy to whom she lent her services, also because she was full of free advice. At the appropriate moment, however, she gathered election votes in favor of the candidates with whom she sided, and from whom she obtained money with much thanks to the elected. The numbers added up and made her patients believe that a strange wheel of fortune in the election had made her a winner every time.

I have an older sister named Alice; she is thirty-one, and since she was eleven has been in a mental hospital due to a mess in which she was involved when she was eighteen. She was a beginning seamstress, and by attending a specialization course she became a capable little caterpillar creating high-quality clothes. In fact, she had made several of my dresses that I was proud to wear, and Alice was proud for having created them. Her dream was to open a shop for repairs and creations of new clothes, but she did not have the financial strength to bear the initial costs. Our parents took the ball and planned a meeting with a family they knew. The purpose was to contract the marriage between Alice and their eldest son, who was looking for a wife. Alice immediately showed her disappointment, and until the date set for the fateful meeting, my parents beat her, forcing her to accept what was imposed on her.

The young man presented himself, accompanied by his parents, who were enthusiastic about describing the dowry that their son could boast. Alice, however, continued to refuse to accept what was proposed, and the meeting did not yield anything but the promise that everything would be adjusted within a few days, and that Alice would eventually accept the future marriage. They decided to meet again in four days, and during this time Alice was the object of more beatings and threats. My parents tried to persuade her, but she never stopped opposing them with all her strength. In the end, after her umpteenth refusal, my mother and father decided to drive her out of the house. I was disturbed when they told me she was leaving home. Alice went to live with my Confirmation godmother, and in the meantime kept busy looking to work for some tailor, at least to make a living, given her talent as a seamstress. I was nine years old then, and I realized that those responsible for that absurd situation in which Alice ended up were undoubtedly my mother and father, who did not like being overruled by their daughter.

They were only used to criticizing others, and on that occasion, they were the ones being criticized. After that episode, Alice, after continuous attempts to find a job, became depressed, sinking into the abuse of alcohol, becoming almost a rag. The depression that gripped her became too much. So, at the insistence of my godmother, my parents agreed to accept her return home. One day, drunk, she went out on the balcony bare-breasted, and screamed out against those who had arranged that marriage. My mother turned to the police. A medical team arrived on the spot, and thanks to her acquaintance with influential people such as the mayor, the specialist made an immediate request for a compulsory medical treatment, which he himself signed without hesitation. As she was dragged off, my sister managed to wriggle away to hug me, and say: "Open your eyes, Maria Clara, spiders are everywhere, and the webs they weave are invisible." The attendants loaded her in an ambulance like a sack of potatoes, and escorted by the traffic police, they took her straight to the asylum.

My mother had finally managed to get rid of her, depositing her in that absurd inhuman parking lot. From that moment on, when my mother wanted to get something from me, she threatened me with the pretext of treating me like Alice, to achieve her wishes. I gave her my obedience in spite of my mistrust. In the missing diary I had written that after middle school, it was my intention to continue studying at high school. She who had stolen my diary, making it disappear, and most likely read it, acted contrarily, enrolling me in the school for nurses that lasted two years. Alice was right. Spider webs really were invisible.

I began to realize this when I moved from class work to my training in medical departments. Some doctors in the ward threatened the trainees with bravado, as they believed they possessed a personal harem. The attendants were not far behind, and the nurses punished the sick, old or young, with the bidet. The men seemed accommodating, but they always stuck close to us; with the excuse of teaching us how to use the syringes, they touched us in subtle ways, trying by every means to win our consent.

There was one, in particular, who, more than the others, insisted on wanting to explore me with his hands. No matter the subject, I always found him as my tutor. His eyes were smiling and hilarious, behind which he hid his silly machismo, and he used his power as a regional union representative to guarantee a job for me after graduation. What he wanted in return was clear, and I busted his balls whenever I felt his advances. He was staring at the four freckles on my face and at the coppery red of my hair. He was convinced that I was the only one to excite him, and that he was taking a break to reflect on his wife whom he was thinking of leaving. The blame for all this he attributed to me, and whispered to me that he loved me, adding that whatever I wanted, he was ready provide for me at any cost. At first, I told him in a polite way to leave me alone, and after his continued insistence I became vulgar, and in a language appropriate to chance, I told him clearly, "Do me a fucking favor, when you are turned on by your wife's blowjobs, stop writing obscene phrases in the doctor's bathroom. Don't deny it; the spelling is yours. You are mentally disturbed." He had swallowed it, and barely ten minutes later he returned, humming the proverb: "Whoever is down is beaten up. Who is down …."

From a colleague of my second year I learned that the year before he tried the same with her friend. She, however, reacted by slapping him. Silvano, so the spider was called, in turn, first had an exaggerated verbal reaction, then tried to harass her by putting his hands under her uniform. The denunciation had no effect whatsoever, since it was initiated by a student against a trade unionist. What they never knew, however, was that the student and her boyfriend, without being recognized, waited for him outside his house and beat him up. He suspected the two, or maybe not, but one thing became certain, he stopped bothering her.

I told my friend that violence was not part of my way of being. I was thinking of what I could to stop him from bothering me. During one shift, we cleaned and put a sick man to bed. Silvano went to organize the dirty stuff in the cart, and I went to the bathroom to empty the bedpan. I rinsed it under running water, filled it, and then placed it on top of the toilet lid. Silvano, not seeing me go out, rushed into the bathroom, closing the door. I stared at him with shining eyes and hissing I said: "We'll see what you are capable of doing." I stood in front of him and he had his back to the door. I pressed my body into him. He replied: "You finally decided to consent." Meanwhile, I loosened his belt, grabbed the bedpan water and poured it into his underwear screaming like crazy. Patients rushed in, I kept screaming, and they opened the door a little at a time. In the meantime, the nun from the ward arrived and soon realized what had happened, and the patients confirmed that they had found me with a messed up uniform. We were called to the health department office and each of us gave our version; the director made the decision to separate us by sending us to different departments. Through this, I resolved the problem of the spider. In the other departments, things did not go any better, since, even if less silly than Silvano, other spiders advanced their moves. They believed that by exercising their power they had the right to make us submit to their desires, their libidinous caprices. Depressed and also unmotivated, I did not want to continue the course, so I quit the boarding school.

My mother did not like my decision and told me: "Now look for a real job. Don't expect anything from me but a place to eat and sleep. Nothing else."

That bitch, in her heart, would have been happy if they had raped me just to see me become a nurse according to her perverse will.

I got a job at a bar, serving customers. I did not know the job, but I soon learned the truth. The customers were terrible tippers, but with a wide hand they proffered obscene proposals, as if I were a whore. The owner of the bar, my employer, was not much better. While I was cleaning the glasses behind the counter sink, he took advantage of me by rubbing my ass, and fingering my back with the hands of his hypocrisy. After just fifteen days he invited me to something else, and he blackmailed me, telling me that if I wouldn't to go along with his erotic temptations he would fire me. I sent him to hell, and he, by reaction, insulted me several times calling me a slut.

I found myself again without a job, and my mother accused me of not being able to bear the suffering and the pressure of my working conditions. Against her judgment, I enrolled in high school. I was aware that because I was older, I would be a fool to other students, but that did not stop me. I studied with passion, because only by passion could I compete with my classmates, and I did everything out of passion. In the afternoon, to get the money necessary to maintain my studies, I served as a babysitter, taking care of twins. My job was to wait for them to come out of pre-school, to take them to the park's merry-go-rounds, bringing them home when their parents returned from their jobs. This young couple was polite and behaved properly. One day, however, because of the lady's husband, this all took a turn for the worse. This two-faced man showed to be other than what he appeared to be. His insolence was such that he even went so far as to demand from me that I gave him access to my cunt. That pig threatened to fire me if I did not accept. I stood up for myself. His reaction was to fire me, justifying himself with his wife by saying that it was me who had provoked and tried to seduce him. He, to prove himself faithful to his wife, ordered me to leave his house immediately. I lost my job again, paying with my skin, for the dirty conscience of others, but for me, this was nothing new.

Only adults, parents or relatives, were allowed to visit the asylum. In Alice's case, she refused visits from her father and mother. My parents began to pay for their misdeeds, and as a result my relationship with them cracked even more. It all started when, leaving home to help to an elderly lady, after walking a couple of blocks, I realized I had forgotten the textbook that I wanted to read. I was forced to go back home to get it where I had carelessly left it. As I went about this, I noticed the light burning in the kitchen and thought to turn it off, since there was nobody at home at that moment. The glass door, however, was closed, even though my mother always left it open and you only had to turn its handle. Intrigued by this novelty, I pushed my gaze beyond the frozen glass, and saw shadows moving. I listened to the voices. I could not fully understand what was said between them, but I seemed to understand that my mother was asking someone to remain calm, that everything would be all right. On hearing this, I slipped out of the apartment. Once in the street, from the booth on the opposite corner, I phoned my client, apologizing in advance, for the long delay in meeting her. After that, I chose an observation point that would allow me to keep an eye on the door of my house without being noticed.

About half an hour later out came two women, more or less between twenty and twenty-five. One held the other, pale in the face, struggling to walk. They took just a few steps then stopped next to a car. Someone from inside opened the rear doors; they entered, and the car left. Thanks to an oversight, that evening I was an involuntary witness of a chilling fact. From then on, I changed my working time by an hour, the time necessary to stand in the usual place and watch the door of my house. The building where I lived had only one floor divided into two apartments, one was us, while the other was empty, which is why, whoever went in and out did it through my mother's and my father's apartment. There wasn't movement every night, but I did not lose heart, I was sure something would happen.

One evening, in fact, it suddenly started to rain, and for shelter, I returned home. On the stairs I took care not to make any noise, and after passing the first floor, I crouched on the first step of the balcony that led to the terrace. Once there, I heard the doorbell ring; the door opened, and more than one person came up. My mother waited for them on the threshold, inviting them to enter; she begged them to sit down, and then closed the door. Nervously, I scrambled down the stairs slowly, leaning against the door.

"She is a minor," said my mother, adding: "You must give me one hundred and fifty thousand lire."

"The one who sends us will pay any expense; the important thing is that you solve the problem," the others answered. That said, they were silent. I did not know what was going on, and I was on the verge of tears.

My mother practiced abortions. She was an executioner in the pay of the well-meaning people educated by esteemed professors, who hid behind false masks. They, with the money they had, bought virgin girls to satisfy their sexual whims, and when they impregnated them, there was my mother and others like her to solve the problems. The girls were naive, also because sex education was a taboo in the schools, and there was no teacher who would speak about it. The education that came with it barely consisted of civic education. True, for pregnant girls there were counselors, but they were like tire repairers who fixed the holes by gluing patches on them.

That evening I wrote three anonymous letters denouncing the incident. The first I addressed to the mayor, the second to social services, and the third to the police. To my mother I could not say a thing, otherwise she would have driven me out of the house, and I had to complete my studies, even though I was already of age. My letters were ignored.

I told all this to Alice the day when, as an adult, I went to visit her. Of our mother, she said: "She's the type of person who gets satisfaction the moment she extorts gossip, like when she hears things like a husband beat his wife. When she's with her friends she's on their side, but later she takes the side of the husband with the excuses that men will always be men. She, however, never let herself be touched with a finger by our father. Regarding the abortions, however, your letters have been ignored because, if you remember well, when you were a child and I hugged you before they sent me here, well, do you remember what I told you? I had to tell you: 'Maria Clara, beware of spiders, their webs are invisible.' Remember, Maria Clara, at nine o'clock, who are the regular customers at their friend's bar? The marshal, the priest, the bank manager, the cops on duty, the architect, the lawyer, the merchant, and some craftsmen. They seem to talk about superfluous things, but each one weaves his own web to capture and devour the victim of the stories and gossip exchanged among them that morning. With the racism they possess, they elaborate plans based on the news they get at nine o'clock the next day in the same bar of the friends."

I understood what Alice was saying. That early morning clique in the bar was a crown in the sunlight, and a mixed brotherhood of pimps and servants hung around them, ready to lend them their services because in due time they would be assured of a job by the clique. Each of them played a role in the prejudice and petty wrangling and also provided, when necessary, false documents for commissions bought that endorsed pensions to fake invalids and those who don't deserve them. These vile and miserable people made their lives in this ugly bad way and couldn't live any other way. Alice had turned to one of these ignoble men of the clique, since many continued to refuse her a job, and she had to work to support herself. The letters of recommendation they issued were a sure guarantee for getting a job. The price of these letters varied according to the employment proposed by the applicant, and in the case of a woman who could not pay with money, in return she had to offer sexual services. Not only that, if the person concerned had not been to their liking, they would have forced her to persuade some friend to take her place in their erotic games. In the absence of all this, their offers also required that the interested parties replace themselves with a minor, considered more attractive. In these cases, the poor women who suffered the abuse sometimes got pregnant, and even on these occasions they had in their ranks complacent mothers who never said a word about it all.

It figures that my letters ended up under the eyes of those who committed such misdeeds. They ended up being immediately trashed. Alice wouldn't accept those absurd conditions, so she spent her last savings getting drunk, until she came to beg for shelter from our parents. They accepted her, more than anything else, so they wouldn't be laughed at by others, as had happened in the past, thinking that at the first stupid act they would simply lock her up in an asylum. Our city is full of these fools, and every neighborhood has a bar that welcomes them. All miseries are analyzed ruthlessly with the intent to derive profits and pleasures from every situation. Leeches that they are, in their neighborhood they feel like royalty.

I, Maria Clara, among the metaphorical ass cocks I took, decided to set up an introspective process for and against myself. I want to vent my thoughts. Who is Maria Clara? Who do you think you are? I have always been an animal, female, with shapes in the right proportion. I'm just looking for the other half of the apple. To be clear, for the male I don't want so much to fuck as I want to be a flower of passion, but above all I seek a mutual understanding based on dialogue and respect. I have always tried, but I have not yet found the right man I want. So, I took care of myself, since adolescence, caressing my pussy with unbridled and delicate passion so that I that deflowered myself. Excited by the images of the eight-millimeter porn movies I saw in a friend's house, I masturbated energetically whenever I went in heat, imagining I had a real cock between my thighs. I was impatient in my imagination because it was I who wished to choose and not to be chosen. In the orgasms in which I was basking, I touched nirvana, humming and declaiming erotic verses.

I always went alone to concerts, preferring singer-songwriters, and it always depended on whether or not I could afford the ticket. Sometimes I went with friends, but now they prefer clubs, and I continue going to the concerts alone.

The songwriters are factories of stories in verse, and together, I think they would form an army of minstrels from the past and from the contemporary world. Bob Dylan, Pino Daniele, and finally the less fortunate Mauro

Lusini are all songwriters who sing about love and the social environment. There are others, such as D'Andrè, for example, but in the end, they all capture the same themes through poetic nuances with different sounds.

I live for poetry. I immerse myself in writing with enthusiasm and I often read cursed poets like Baudelaire or Rimbaud, and accursed contemporaries, like the writers of the Beat Generation. As far as I'm concerned, for years I've been writing poems and stories, drawing inspiration from my life and the everyday facts that surround me. I kept them all in order, so that one day it occurred to me publish my work. I studied about my possibilities, drawing the conclusion that I could send my typescripts to the various publishing houses in the hope that at least one would publish my works. The many responses I received seemed to come from the same source, as they were identical and standard, such as: "Poetry is a niche market, and it sells very little." The critiques of my stories, however, spoke of retrograde or futuristic themes that the public did not like. In short, every judgment was negative, telling me my narrative was out of place in these times.

These continuous rejections would discourage anyone who has a minimum of talent and believes in what he writes, not least because there are no great writers around. In bookstores there are shelves of books to browse, you realize that the only thing of value is the cover with the title and the logo of the publishing house. In the face of all this, I was never discouraged. I tried again to be published, and this time with the cash contribution that was requested. The editors, however, always required exorbitant amounts that I couldn't afford. Only one accepted, and did not even want a penny, but in return demanded that I offer him my body. I sent him to hell with a loud fuck you. As he came out of his office, slamming the door, his secretary winked at me, with a big smile, she flashed me a thumbs up. I had fallen into a labyrinth, and I needed an Ariadne to come out of it, but I felt like a Penelope in war, paraphrasing the title of a book written by Fallaci. So, I insisted on writing, thinking that if I had talent, the book would speak for itself. In this regard, I had doubts, because if a book is not printed, how would it be able to talk?

I was struggling with these doubts, suffering through a thousand possible explanations, while in the book store, three titles by the same author appeared in a short time. How was that possible? I knew that author and he had nothing that resembles talent. I am sure that his secret is the banknote, and that he had bought the publisher's yes. Grumpy and snobby before he published, he had never set foot in a bookstore. He had the bookseller put his books in the window in plain sight, and then would observe them from outside, swelling his chest. He was determined and able to weave his dark plots, and bothered the people with begging, at all costs, for them to read his beautiful books; he even offered them to me, knowing I had noticed them at times in the bookstore. He did not know, however, that I involuntarily had read his writings before publication. He had asked for criticism from qualified people who, due to his insistence, and just to satisfy him, agreed to look at his work, even in the street, if that was the case, and not only that. He bombarded the unfortunate examiners with phone calls the day after they had promised to read his typescripts in their home, or he bothered them on the street urgently requesting their judgment. Among these accidental examiners came my friend Lorenza who, tired of being harassed by him, turned to me for help. She told me that the alleged author in question did not know either grammar or syntax, and that his bad writing was confusing and delirious. I read the manuscripts at the insistence of Lorenza, and agreed with her judgment; they were disconnected, ungrammatical and perhaps stolen from who knows where. Later Lorenza told me that he had also bothered others like her, and that after collecting the various judgments all negative, he ignored them. He took his work and had them printed.

When the books were published, they say he did nothing but give them away to those who pleased him or had acceded to his shady designs as a writer. He also gave them to all those who had read his manuscripts and had given him negative responses; he did this all with a spirit of revenge, according to what Lorenza told me. I told him I didn't want to hear about his books. From then on, he targeted me by continuing to torture me with his convictions, almost harassing me. One day I couldn't take it any longer and so I told him: "Open your ears well. What I will tell you will either make you squirm with rage or make you laugh. One thing is certain, however, the substance in your head is the same that you publish in your books. I say it frankly: I envy your products, I feel envy for you. Now you can get angry or laugh, the important thing is that you get off my back."

Halfway through the diary, I noticed that a page from a local magazine had been glued in, preceded by this introduction:

After so much running around, a local magazine, after I had bought a subscription, published my story inspired by a newspaper account. Embittered by the frequency of similar degenerative phenomena in the social world, I wrote this story entitled "Carlotta."

"I'm here, in an old hotel. Lying on one of the beds in the room, I am drunk on beer and my mouth reeks of nicotine. I smoke constantly and stare at the ceiling. Squalor reigns, like my mood. My nerves are shot, and I really want to cry. Rust has no time to waste and it covers me more and more quickly. Finally, the dearest and saddest memory is you, Carlotta, the reflection and epicenter of these my visions.

"I relaxed on the train. From the window, I saw trees and houses darting by. The rapid play of light and shadows made me nervous; I pulled down the shade and tried to rest. I was thinking about you, Carlotta, intensely, until my head began to burst. I read your address and wondered if it was false. You hadn't left two hours early, as you had made me believe. You were born and lived in that city. I got off the train at the first stop and waited for the connection to arrive. I saw you in the park. I listened to you exchanging lewd phrases for a few bills. You absolutely had to collect the amount necessary to buy your dreams.

'Do you have a thousand lire?'

'Why?' I replied. That was how our ephemeral and intense friendship was born.

'Who are you to ask me why? Are you my mother? You told me about your generation, the Beatles, Bob Dylan, and Allen Ginsberg. In the first poems you wrote, you were inspired by them because, at the time, the book market offered these authors. You know what the market offers me? Only used condoms. I find them outside the school gates.'

'Which school?'

'Middle School. Where else?'

'My God! How old are you?

'Why should I tell you?

'Imagine if they had asked you for your I.D. in the hotel where we slept? They would have thrown me in jail too.'

'But this didn't happen, so you should be happy.'

'No, Carlotta. I've taken our friendship seriously from the start.'

'No, I say so. To me, you are only one of the many lost objects that I have collected and kept for myself as long as I thought necessary. I wanted to make friends with you and did it. Don't blame me If you think you're a philanthropist.'

'All that tenderness and desire that you showed, was it fictitious?'

'In those moments I was honest. I care about friendship. Call them moments, call them years, call them centuries, even you poets never measure time, but I assure you that in friendship I always give my soul. Now, if you do not mind, let me go.'

'Yeah, it's easy for you. You know that with age you find yourself; you have lost all your values, and you did it quickly.'

'Think of it as you wish, but leave me alone. After all, who do you think you are? You're just a poet who goes around selling poems. You are a poet disguised as a tough guy, and not at all alternative. That's enough, let me go.'

It all happened in a rush: a flame under the spoon and a vacuum with the syringe, then straight into the vein, and goodnight. I stood there looking and crying. Could I do something? I sat on the sidewalk and wrote. Shortly after, I called you, but you were on the road. You put the paper in your pocket and I went away crying, leaving you under the porticoes with your companions in misfortune. Six months later, I read the news on page two.

'Carlotta Di Venere dead by an overdose. She was fifteen.'

There were two photos attached to the article. The first one showed you smiling, and the second one was slightly bigger. Really, did one have to see the poor body as it had been found! Then came the speeches of the various moralists. I must live with the thought of not having done anything to save you.

The last time I went to visit Alice, I was stunned. She told me she wanted to stay in that place until death had caught her. She no longer wanted to have anything to do with her family. She preferred to stay with madmen. In truth, and I knew it by way of crossroads, in that place she had recently met a friend of misfortune, Annalisa, who also went mad because of people's judgments and rumors. She had been engaged, and everything went smoothly, until the boy's parents learned that she had a handicapped brother in the family. The prejudices and beliefs of the usual ignoramuses suggested that a possible son of the two future spouses would be born handicapped. Persuaded by these superstitions they began to sow discord and managed to tear the relationship between the two engaged couples. The boy found another woman, while Annalisa lost her way and took the short cut, voluntarily choosing the asylum, accentuating her madness; severing her relations with the outside world had caused her so much harm. Annalisa and Alice were united by the same fate, and if the idea of seeing my sister locked up forever saddened me, it seemed natural for me to accept her decision.

The following pages were thicker than others. Here were some reprints of a national magazine which dealt with mystical subjects and arcane themes: mystery, fantasy, and magic. There was another story.

Very Cold

"The intercom cawed like a crow. Adele woke with a start, and got out of bed, stepped into her slippers and walked quickly to the corridor that led to the entrance, where the intercom continued its hoarse crackling. She grabbed the phone and asked, 'Who is it?'

'Sorry, Adele, I left and forgot my keys,' someone replied. 'Take a look. They should be on the desk.'

'Which desk? There is no desk here,' and then she asked, 'Who is it?'

'What? Who is it? I'm Giuseppe, your husband. Come on, look for them quickly, otherwise how can I start the car and get to the clinic? Come on, don't make me come up; just throw them out the window.'

'Sir,' the woman insisted, 'I do not know you, and why I should look out the window and throw you the keys?'

'Listen, Adele, I left just two minutes ago, I kissed you and you slept like a log. I said goodbye to the children, kissing them too and I went out forgetting the keys upstairs.'

'Children? There are no children here. There's no desk.'

'Tonia and Nico, what happened to them?'

'Sir, you're definitely mistaken. Tonia and Nico are almost fifteen years old, so they are not children. My husband died ten years ago. So, if you are pretending to be him, don't try to force me to believe you are him.'

So saying, Adele looked up at the corner of the wall in front of her. There sat a framed photo of her husband, who had died ten years earlier. Above a small table under the painting, was a small lit lamp and a container with flowers, and next to the glass, a small note with an epitaph written in large letters. Over the intercom the man's voice kept insisting that Adele should open the door, and from the tone one could sense that his was not, after all, an absurd presumption.

'Okay,' the man continued to say with a certain concentration. 'I know very well that we had a fight last night, but there is no need for drama. Don't pretend you don't understand, and please open the door.'

'My God! I repeat, you are wrong. My husband died in a car accident ten years ago.'

'No,' said the man, 'I am your husband and I am alive and well, and I warn you that if you do not open immediately, I'll start screaming.'

Tonia was going to the bathroom when she noticed her mother on the phone. She asked with whom she was speaking, and her mother tried to explain the strange situation that had arisen.

'There's a guy who says he's your father and wants to come up.'

'To do what?' responded the daughter.

'I don't know. He says he forgot the keys.'

'But if Dad is dead, how come he is down at the door?'

'Who's talking about dead?' Shouted a voice from the other room. It was Nico who had woken up.

'Adele,' screamed the man, 'what's going on? Why, don't you let me in?'

'Lord, be patient. I'll be down in a couple of minutes so we can clear up this incredible thing.'

In a blink of an eye the woman washed her face, dressed quickly, and went down to the door. She opened the door and at that moment the man turned his back, and as soon as he turned, Adele stood looking at him stony. The one in front of her was the spitting image of Giuseppe. The same eyes, the same hair, the same height; he even wore the same clothes he had worn on the day of the accident. He looked her in the eye and said: 'What is this story of the accident and the dead? I understand you're still angry at last night's discussion, but it seems to me you're exaggerating. I begged your forgiveness. Wasn't that enough for you? Do you want me to start begging you? Now my relationship with Linda is part of the past and it will not happen again; I also explained why. Since I told you this story, though, you've only been teasing me. Last night, for the umpteenth time, you wanted to know how the facts went. I told them all, but apparently, you still are not convinced that I told you the truth. I'm ready to tell it again, that story, but I swear, this is the last time I do it.

'After graduating med school, I was practicing in the hospital. Along the way, in addition to the staff and the students, there was a girl who struck me in particular. I met her one day when I went to take the place of a doctor who was doing anatomy and physiology lessons. I noticed her from the first moment I had set foot in the classroom, and, even then, something magical hovered in the air. I felt attracted to that woman. Her thin, delicate, rosy-cheeked face often baffled me. I stood staring at her eyes, small, and very often hidden by her curly hair, so much so that it was difficult to find them; everyone was aware of the interest I showed towards that woman.

'Linda watched my hands, mostly affected by the movements. My deftness with my fingers was the object of her gaze, and her questions came more often. In the ward, she was a geek, and many took advantage of her availability and her altruism. They were abusing her, but she never gave in to them; she continued to work conscientiously. She was never afraid to ask about what she could not understand. One day, by an unusual coincidence, it was up to me to satisfy her curiosity. She was enthusiastic and grateful; she grabbed my hand to thank me. She had never done that!

'I felt every part of my skin assaulted by a pleasant sensation. I felt so good that, although I felt chills, I hoped that that moment would never end. From that day on, we always found excuses to talk to each other, and being together became a need for us. We were of the same zodiac sign and we had many things in common. The only thing that made me sick was the difference in age between me and her. She confided everything to me and could not keep even the smallest of secrets to herself. Once she told me about a friend of hers who was a poet who was courting her. This friend of his wrote wonderful poems reciting them on the radio and dedicating them to her, so much so that this way of doing things had disturbed her for a long time. Who knows for what obscure reason, ever since she had told me about this poet, I remembered a great and famous author of the past and rediscovered the joy of rereading his poems. At a certain point, as I read, I had a foreboding, so much so that, during our usual conversations, I asked Linda if she knew and had read something about that great poet. She did not know him. I told her that he was one of the founders of the Beat Generation, and I promised to let her read one of his best-known books. Linda looked at me intently. I felt I had known what she was thinking. Meanwhile the bus arrived. I accompanied her to the bus stop and, just before going upstairs, she moved her mouth close to my ear and said, "For a moment, I wanted you to kiss me."

'It was just that, the thought I had perceived. I was happy, and sad at the same time, as I walked towards my car parked near the train station. There I opened the door, sat behind the wheel, bent my head, and with my hands in my hair I tried to think calmly. I reflected on the sense of emptiness that suddenly roamed impatiently inside my conscience. I thought of you, dear wife. I thought of our children, and the eyes that I should use to look at you. I tried to find, unsuccessfully, the way to tell you that I was in love with Linda. After all, why should I have told you, if I had not even realized myself that I was in crisis? A few days later I decided to bring Linda the great poet's book. I went to see her in the classroom during the break between one lesson and another. Linda stood with her hands resting on the radiator attached to the wall; she had not seen me enter because she was warming herself; her back was facing me. I surprised her and held the book before her eyes. She gave a start and said hello. I said goodbye, then she grabbed the book, began to leaf through it, and finally read a random poem. What happened soon after, just thinking about it, gives me goosebumps.

'Suddenly, seized by a crisis, she slammed the book over the desk shouting:

'Why in the world are there always wolves hunting for lambs?' With the speed of lightning, she burst into tears and ran out of the classroom. I let her run, I thought it was right to stay awhile alone with herself.

'Finally, after thinking about it, I was able to understand something of what she would later tell me when she returned to the classroom. The poems that the friend recited for her had been in large parts plagiarized by the book in question. I imagined the anguish Linda felt in those moments, however, I left her with that bad feeling, because I knew I could not help her. One evening, a few days later, waiting for her to leave the hospital, I asked if she wanted my company as far as the bus; she said yes with enthusiasm. After a few meters she took my hand in hers and let me lead her where she wanted without saying anything, like a happy child. We found ourselves in a small street, lit only by a small light bulb placed in a corner. Linda had a strange light in her eyes. She looked at me intently and said:

'Don't you feel it in the air? ....''

'I answered yes. We both waited for that moment, and finally it had arrived! I kissed her very gently. Rapid and tender caresses ran through our faces, and overwhelmed by those feelings with a whisper, I murmured: 'This sweet moment is ours alone, no one can deny it to us.'

I realized then that we found ourselves falling in love, and a moment later, we had lost it. After that evening, everything happened as though nothing had happened, and among us only friendship remained. A few months later Linda graduated, and from that day on I never saw her again. I understood well that I had lost her forever.

'This is my sin, dear Adele. Now, if you do not mind, I need to get to work. I want this day all for myself; I want to go where I want, even if it's to hell.'

Suddenly flames appeared that set fire to and colored the wall of oblivion. Adele woke with a start and jumped out of bed, running into the bathroom. She put her head under the tap and let the water flow. She only pulled back when she was sure she had woken up completely. Meanwhile, Tonia left her bed and ran into her parents' room. After kissing her little brother who slept, she turned to the other side of the bed and called: 'Dad, get up! Today, it's your turn to take us to kindergarten. Wake up, come on, mom is already in the bathroom. Pappa, Pappa. Mommy! Daddy is very cold?'"

At the end of this story, a long missive began on the following page. It was a letter from the editor of the magazine, and said:

> *Dear Reader,*
>
> *I took note of the letter you sent me about the story published in No. 60 of our magazine entitled "Very Cold." I inform you that each author assumes responsibility for the authenticity of the work. From what has been verified by your communication, you claim to have sent the work in question to a literary consultant and friend, and that through her negligence she confused it with the drafts of the author you have questioned who is the subject of any plagiarism claimed by her. In addition, she claims that the consultant of both found in her mailbox the n/s magazine on which had been attached a note with the words: "Envy must die." We requested the truth from your friend and consultant, and she responded with proper and legitimate clarifications to our editorial staff. I remind you that these particular cases, and any consequent disputes, are the subject of judgment by a competent court.*
>
> *As director of this cultural magazine, I assure you that, the author contacted by us in turn has not received any money in exchange, and that, with this author, there are no contractual obligations of any kind. With the certainty of what I have said, I take this opportunity to invite you to submit future works that relate to our magazine's philosophy.*

Sincere and best regards

The director
Lionello Londo

Here I was, in the present with twenty-two years inside, outside, and behind me, transmitted and written on an electrocardiograph paper roll: tachycardias, bradycardias, fibrillations, and long pauses. My heart had been empty of atropine and adrenaline. The sound of that violin was for my being the shock of a defibrillator, and I was woken out of my hibernation. I felt like a stone thrown into the water. The concentric circles moved away and then returned to the same point where stunned, I watched the ebb and flow of events in a swamp defined as civil society.

The Penelope that was in me licked the wounds still open from the defeats, and her screams were soap bubbles that rose floating to the water's surface. Now awake, your thin face appeared to me with two hollow eyes, long, pitch black hair. You were wrapped in a harness of barbed wire that stung you. It was your skein, and I felt the pain you felt. We shared the same pain caused by introspection. Which of us spoke first? I was struggling, trying to remember. I had a memory, though, and it was my only thought of you. I had the feeling that you were a Siddhartha in search of the truth to get rid of the pains of the world, or the struggle between good and evil that was in each of us as in the novel Dr. Jekyl and Mr. Hyde. I saw the struggle between life and death in you, and the winner was hooded and carried a scythe. This image of you, which I had before my eyes, reminded me of a world where the prevarications, the hatred, the falsehoods, the violence and the absurd doctrines of the war no longer happened.

Your paintings fascinate me, disturb me, my conscience oscillates, so I can't tell if I'm good or bad. The brushstrokes of your landscapes resemble those of the French impressionists, but you are self-taught, and your strength is spontaneity; painting for you is a liberating act. Your seascapes probably express your anger, your hidden anxieties, a wave that is the flow of your life and your pains. The olive trees with twisted branches in turn suggest to me arms which open to nothing, only branches, but one in particular looks like Atlas on his knees supporting the planet on his shoulders.

There is no peace in your painting, dawns and sunsets arise and die among tumultuous, restless skies. Dear Van Gogh, for artists, the century in which we are born is never the right one. I, who belong to the artistic world with my poetic and narrative contributions, continue to pay my dues, and arrested within me is the factory of creativity that the world attaches to me with its seals. In this situation I am inclined to abandon the monotony of Ithaca to venture with you on an Odyssey. You, with brushes and colors, I with my notebooks, and I would like our mission to be that we both create. Most likely, we will not have enough money to live, but only survive with dignity. I would also like to give and receive love in equal measure. I would like to have your sex inside me, enjoy it and let you enjoy me. There is no more authentic union of sex practiced than intimate love. I know you will not disappoint me, I'm not a clairvoyant, but I have a sensitive soul that allows me to predict my vicissitudes in love as in life. Open your colors, as I open my pains in this diary, so we will kill the ghost who haunts us, with only rainbows inside and outside us.

N.B. I include the verses written immediately after our first meeting:

"Thoughts of an April evening"

I saw his eyes
wander into nothingness,
looking for something.
I saw purity, anguish,
sadness and anger.
His face hid
a cry without tears.

I read the diary in full over three days and nights. The confessions of Maria Clara made my thoughts jump. The ink of the pages became an endless flash, before the thunder, in my eyes. All this shattered the silence in which, I, the recipient of her confessions, had entrenched myself. In the fragmentation the question arose as to why the sense of the diary had become a trench for me. Then in the calm the answer hit me; there was not a war declared in that diary, but a frank declaration of love. The *capotosta*, if anything, was me, I could hardly believe it. I repeated by heart the many readings in which I had tried, almost as if I were declaiming the words, to convince myself that what I thought was the truth. In the end, there were two questions: either I had lifted Maria Clara from her genuflections, or I had to genuflect myself. In both cases, our relationship was to be born in balance.

The same evening, despite the late hour, I had the urge to go to her house. I pushed the intercom button, and the door opened. As soon as I crossed the threshold, someone slammed a door and came down the stairs quickly, shouting:

"I want to see you face to face."

Her mother stood before me and yelled, "Ah! It's you, the hero. The stupid girl is in love with a man like you? Well, look at you! You know, champion, that just today I kicked your girl out of your house. You don't have to come here anymore. That vagabond must sleep in the open."

I did not utter a word, and when I left, I thought of going to where my friend gave her private lessons. The door was shut, and a sign had been posted on it: For Rent. I had no idea where to look for her, and with a storm in my head, I slowly returned to the guesthouse where I was staying.

A woman sat on the steps of the main entrance. On her knees she had a big rucksack where her head rested. My heart was beating, and when I was near her, the woman raised her head and looked me in the eye. It was Maria Clara! I leaned in front of her, and with the look of a lover in amazement I told her, "I was at your house and at the club, and I heard what happened to you. Frankly, I let myself be carried away by my doubts for having decided too late to take you with me."

I grabbed her hands gently and held her up, pulling her towards me. We hugged each other and kissed, pushing past the unknowns. The kisses and the caresses were the wings that hovered above us, and soon we glided up, then back down with our feet on the ground.

"I've been here for two hours. I did not know where to look for you anymore," said Maria Clara.

"It took a while to get your house and then to where you give your lessons," I replied.

"I've been around since the early afternoon. I wandered around the city. I was also at Lorenza's, and I didn't realize the time that passed. When I got here, I immediately rang your bell, but nobody was there. So, I decided to sit here waiting for you to come back. I thought, among other things, that you too have the right to attend to your business."

"Come on, let's go in, you're soaked. Give me the backpack; I'll carry it in."

Once inside my room Maria Clara sat on a chair, while I rested my backpack on the bed asking her, "Is it true that she kicked you out?"

"No. I was the one who left with full freedom, with my feet. Then, at the club, did you see the sign?"

"Yup."

"Fortunately, with Lorenza, we discovered that the landlord to whom we have paid the rent is not the rightful owner, but one who pretends to be so. In reality, he ran a fruit and vegetable shop on the corner of our block. Last week we tracked down his wife. We found out, talking to her, that her husband was collecting the rent on behalf of the owner. She also said that they too paid the lease for their shop to that gentleman, and that he would show up soon. He presented himself this morning. Lorenza got there before I did. Anyway, I have just glimpsed the owner who at that moment turned the corner of the greengrocer after talking with Lorenza, and I recognized him as my father. Lorenza, in turn, told me that he was asked to increase the rent to thirty thousand lire a month. He had replied that he would consult with his partner and then give her the definitive answer. Meanwhile, Lorenza had signed the lease with the greengrocer who was therefore only an agent. The owner who demanded the increase did not want to enter into a new contract, most likely because he had found a new tenant. After that, I told Lorenza that the owner was my father. At this point, Lorenza and I left the room leaving all the furniture and bringing with us only what that belonged to us."

I listened to her story intently trying to figure it all out, so I asked her, "Then what happened?"

"I rushed home, grabbed my things and threw them in a shopping bag and backpack. I then left the keys on the table writing a note:

We are all destined to die, build a monument in the cemetery and fill it with money, because you do not know where to put it. Go and fuck yourselves.

Your renter of Via Cadorna 56.
Maria Clara

"Going down the stairs I met my mother climbing up. I immediately told her that her daughter's resignation was on the table, and that I had had enough. Here I am, now, Sebastiano, and I hope you can host me."

"Of course, I can host you. The bed is there, always if you agree to sleep with me, otherwise there is the sofa bed."

She nodded, and in her eyes, there was a moment of tranquility, so that it seemed to me that she already thanked me in advance. So, naturally, I spoke to her sincerely about what I was able to understand from the pages of her diary and spontaneously told her, "From what I could understand from the diary I read, you have a high regard for me, and you have immense trust in me. I hope, from here on out, to be strong enough to handle whatever comes our way. The future, after all, is nothing but a score of an opus already written, but we both don't yet know how to read the music. You can't have and know everything in life. We will therefore bite the bullet, if necessary, and go forward with determination; they will bend us, but they will not be able to break us; we will be like rushes in the wind. I really hope for this."

I saw that she had listened to me attentively, as if the things I had told her were what she had also thought. This led me to push further, and I told her, "Your poems, your stories denounce but do not scratch the reality of facts that surpasses even every human fantasy. My paintings, however, denounce, without half measures, the malaise that grips my life. After I vomit my colors, the peace never lasts long, and anxiety grows again. So, I start fighting with the weapons I have: paints, a palette and brushes."

Meanwhile, in my room, which was an attic, I opened the door that led to the terrace, and a gust of wind melted our eyes. Maria Clara awoke first from the hypnosis of the words and told me: "Look! The moon travels the same orbit in the sky." Against the door we turned our backs on the moon, while she added, "Those mirrors, why are they in the corner?"

"To reflect the light coming from the glass window, the only place where light enters in this attic, since the door is a solid wood panel. Thanks to the reflected light I can paint as if I were outdoors."

"The canvases lined up one after the other and showing the unpainted slice; why are they arranged like that?"

"If every painting was in plain sight I would run the risk of looking at it continuously, paralyzing myself, and this weakens and sometimes even blocks the flow of my creativity."

"Ah!" She answered, looking like someone who wanted to consider someone with genuineness and frankness. I watched her carefully, and suddenly I said: "I think you too are starving. Should we grab a pizza? What do you want?"

"Yes, I am hungry, but I don't want to go down the stairs; the day's been draining; I'm tired."

"I'll bring it here, do not worry, just tell me how you like it."

"I don't have any particular tastes. You choose for me."

"In the meantime, if you don't like the quiet you can turn on the radio. It's an FM, and if you want, try to tune in to the Radio Rondine station. Ciao, I'll see you soon."

I left the pizzeria with two pizza boxes, a bag with two three-quarter-liter bottles, one of beer and the other of wine, and headed for the guesthouse. In a flash I went up the stairs, and when I was in front of the door, I knocked hard with my feet, drawing the attention of Maria Clara, who promptly opened the door for me. The table had been set, and the mess had disappeared. I put my things on the table, we sat down, unpacking and opening the bottles, we started to dine, enjoying our pizza. Radio Rondine played songs, and the radio host, lowering the music from time to time, reminded the audience that the music was from the sixties, and that night, like the others, they were playing the revival program dedicated to the truck driver, the taxi driver, and anyone who was busy on the night shift at his workplace, including whores.

At the end of the dinner I went out on the terrace to smoke a cigarette, and five minutes later I was watching Maria Clara strut before the mirrors. A white camisole barely covered her thighs, and she was embarrassed. I felt attracted to her beauty, and with difficulty I approached my desire for her body. I could not find the words to ask her to make love, but words weren't needed. Our bodies were already talking to each other, and instinctively we looked into each other's eyes, caressed each other, hugged and kissed each other. Then I untied the braid wrapped around the back of her head, and her hair like coil springs descended on her shoulders. Only the sound of a violin was missing, as in our first meeting.

Just then, the radio played "For Elise," moving her, perhaps, to moments of her adolescence. Then the rhythms became more frenetic, accelerating, like our hearts. The adagio covered with words, said: "Passion flower in my heart." The excitement broke down the last wall of timidity, opening the doors of pleasure, while outside the door the moon watched over the remains of the night.

Maria Clara was asleep. On the first piece of paper I could find, I wrote a note telling her I was going out to get our breakfast and that I would return as soon as possible; then, hurrying, I went down to get to the nearest bar. At the landing of the lower floor the owner of the attic was waiting for me. I greeted him as always, but on this occasion, he seemed to want to tell me something, and, in fact, he told me, "About your guest, if it's a few nights, it's fine, otherwise you add a supplement to the monthly rent." I accepted his new condition without batting an eyelid and continued up the stairs.

In the street, I went first to the tobacconist for cigarettes and telephone tokens. From the first booth I found open, I phoned the shop to tell my employer that I would be late that morning. He did not answer, not even the second time. A little annoyed, I pressed the button to recover the tokens. I left the booth, headed to the bar, only to find it closed. I was forced to go elsewhere, and two blocks away I bought breakfast, then returned to Maria Clara. The bed where I left her asleep was empty, but the sounds of the water from the bathroom indicated that she had already risen. I called out to let her know I was there, but she couldn't hear me, as she was humming to herself.

The door of the terrace was open, and the sun struck the mirrors that reflected its light. The easel that served as a lectern for her diary attracted my attention because it showed two pages on which a red ink stood out. I read the contents: "Someone has already said that in adolescence everyone writes poetry, but then poets and jerks continue to write it. This is just a cliché; I want to express what's inside me. Believe me, Sebastiano, dirty or clean, this poem is for you, keep it forever. It cost me to write it, even if the first night with you deserves even more and you have entered me drop by drop, and I am mentally humming rain and tears, and between rain and tears there is no difference."

A long and tender kiss
Was our antipasto.
Our lips wanted more.
The curtain closed
Leaving the human trash
backstage.
and we on the stage of the attic.
The bed away from the wall,
the table pushed behind the door
and among the messed-up furniture
our meal started.
The cuddles were sublime.
We, with burning senses;
explorers of ourselves.
Our tongues took off.
Your mouth on my breast
licked my nipples.
Your hands between my thighs
pushed my knees to give way.
You, in front of me,
behind me, above me,

below me, and finally
inside me.
Overturned and upside down
your tongue savored
the honey of my vagina.
My mouth welcomed
your member until
it lost its strength
ejaculating.
Without customary words,
satisfied and not,
in the garden of the empire of the senses
we have walked the avenues.
The interval was
a window closed on the past,
and after the point, started again.

The mirror reflects
my grimaces of pleasure
while breath on grass stems,
how I wanted to burn it,
and my hands tighten
the edges of the mattress.
The mirror insists on returning
pleasure to our eyes!

The game accelerates its rhythm
and suddenly your member
erupts white lava

like a volcano,
and then it stops.

Now we are out of the magic of this night. You left, and I wrote my
feelings on these pages from my mind. So went our first night, with the moon
outside the door, which did what it could to witness all the lovers in the world.

The shop gate was closed, and given the time, I wondered what had happened, trying to figure out why no one had answered my phone calls. I opened the shop with the keys I had been given. Everything was in order as always, and calmly I began to perform the first operations of work. After just five minutes, the phone rang. It was the owner who informed me that he was in the emergency room and asked me to join him as soon as possible. I was putting on my shirt when the phone rang again. I grabbed the phone and answered. Maria Clara told me that she would go to Lorenza to discuss their work and future projects. After her phone call, aware of who was waiting for me, I closed the door of the shop and went to the hospital. Once there, the first-aid nurse pointed to the recovery room, where Master Saverio was under observation. Sitting on a wheelchair, he had an arm immobilized by some bandages, and his face was scraped up and swollen.

"I fell down the stairs of the house," he told me loudly after he saw me coming. Master Saverio looking around with a circumspect air, lowered his tone and with courage he murmured, "The truth is that I was beaten by two strangers. Sebastiano, for years I've been the victim of blackmail. My business is a boon for these criminals. One day a very distinguished gentleman, without too many words, convinced me that I needed a loan in cash for a month. To make a long story short, I took the money and he threatened to disturb my peace of mind if I did not. Right on schedule, he returned the next month with the same pretensions, and for the second time, fifty thousand lire were taken out of my pocket. Every month he was punctual in collecting his sum which, to be honest, I reluctantly gave him."

I listened to the words of my employer feeling a sense of hidden anger, partly because I feared repercussions on me; meanwhile Master Saverio continued to let off steam, "A few months later, an elegant woman entered the shop. She calmly looked over the oldest furniture, and I asked her if I could help her. She replied: 'Beautiful furniture!'

"'You mean this?' I added. She said contemptuously, 'We are looking at the furniture and the shop.'

"I understood the insinuation and told her that there was already someone watching me in exchange for money. She did not get upset, and with a gallant face told me, 'In addition to the shop, we also guarantee the safety of your family.' I surrendered to her blackmail with another fifty thousand lire."

"Mastro Saverio, this is incredible!" I said, interrupting him, but he did not seem to listen to me, and he continued, "Every month, after that, there were two of them coming to me to claim money. They came on Sunday when you were not there, the first in the morning, and the other at noon. These two leeches kept the neighborhood activities in check. Also, during the holidays they phoned me asking that I accommodate their requests for food."

"I'm embittered by what you're telling me," I told him with a concern that grew more and more in me and on my face as I listened. Mastro Saverio meanwhile did not stop and added, "Of course, neither my family nor you were informed of the infamy of these dry-faced people who were nourished by the sweat of others. Do you remember two months ago? A fire broke out at the hardware store near our shop. The owner had been beaten a few weeks before and had reported it. The consequences were tragic; they set fire to his shop. I have always paid them punctually, and I do not think they were the ones who beat me. The other day, after you stopped working and you left, I was about to close when a boy, maybe sixteen, entered the shop. I thought he was looking for a job, but instead he boldy demanded I take a loan from his family. I replied that I had already made two loans, but he with a threatening face said, 'What's that got to do with it? It will mean that instead of two there will be three loans. You can very well handle all three of them.' I ignored his requests, and the consequences of my decision can be seen on my body; they almost killed me. After they beat me up, one said that they were people who kept their word and that within thirty days the same boy would return. In case of insolvency on my part, they would try something else. Sebastiano, at this point I no longer pay a penny to anyone, I am going to close the business and disappear from circulation. In thirty days I will be able to find the right solution. As for your position, let's try to find an agreement. You have been employed by me for five years, and I owe you about four thousand lire more or less. I can give you three hundred in cash, the rest I'll cover with the delivery van. It is in excellent condition, despite being a bit old-fashioned."

"I have a driver's license, but until now I have never driven a vehicle," I replied.

He told me, "Go to a driving school, get some practice, and the problem will be solved."

At that moment the wife of Master Saverio entered into the room. She was coming to bring her husband home. Meanwhile, with both of them preparing to leave, Master Saverio told me, "Anyway, meet me in the shop. We'll deliver the latest works, and that's all. You, meanwhile, let me know if my conditions, for the end of the relationship, are good for you. Take your time."

I went home that evening, and on the stairs I heard Maria Clara singing *Bohème* by Charles Aznavour. I thought it was the perfect song for the uncertainty of our future. Entering the house, I did not distract her from singing and later told her everything that was boiling in the pot.

"Let's reason calmly, you'll see, we'll find a solution," she replied with great confidence.

The next day, on Friday, as if nothing had happened, out of habit I went to work. Mastro Saverio was there with his wife and said to me, "Finish waxing these two small tables, let them dry, and then close everything. Tomorrow, do not come, and do not worry; I'll pay you as though you worked. See you on Monday."

At midday, Maria Clara was surprised to see me at lunch. I explained the reasons for it, and finally we realized that we had two and a half days at our disposal. Meanwhile, I noticed that Maria Clara had arranged my canvases one on top of the other based on the measurements and kept at it. She stared at them, then grabbed one and as she carried it in she told me: "I have already moved the canvases that were out on the terrace under the canopy; it is amazing in that one the seagull seems to want to fly out of the picture. In any case, let's gather all the paintings so we can count them and know for sure how many there are."

She began to count them patiently and finally said to me: "You have a capital of seventy paintings."

"We have capital," I replied with conviction, and then added, "you choose ten, and we will try to sell them." So, late in the afternoon we went to a gallery owner who bought three paintings, then another gallery took two, and the price was acceptable from both. By the time we got home that evening, we had five fewer paintings and two hundred thousand lire, and so we planned to spend the weekend outside the city. On Sunday morning we boarded the first train south. We had no destination. For two hours we did nothing but look out the window at endless rows of vineyards. At one point the landscape changed. Olive trees took the place of the vineyards, and this fascinated Maria Clara, who yelled out, "Let's get off at the next stop."

Once the train left, we realized that the station was in open country. We found out from other travelers that the countryside was two kilometers from the station. We did not follow the directions we received and set out for winding dirt roads that went through the countryside. Thick rows of olive trees, almonds, and cherries accompanied us on our journey; we walked until, almost tired, we took a path that led to two columns of a long road. At the bottom was an abandoned farmhouse that attracted our attention. Only peace and quiet reigned there, and from the farmyard, with a few short steps, we found ourselves under a pergola. Here there was a large slab of stone resting on two trunks, upon which, perhaps, the owner had lunch outside.

We pulled out the few supplies from our backpacks and made a quick breakfast. While we ate, we looked around and noticed that an old tower stood about a mile away, at the top of which there was a small wrought-iron cross. We gathered our things into the backpack. We made our way slowly, one tree at a time, to the foot of the tower. The place was deserted, and we easily pushed open the tower's door. The inside measured more or less nine square meters. There was a staircase, formed by the protruding stones of the façade, and below, in a corner, bundles of dried branches, a few small trunks, and two sacks of straw were piled up, nothing else. The tower did not have a roof, and if there once was one, it certainly had collapsed because looking up you could see the sky.

In that vibrant peace and quiet, immersed in the nature of the countryside, neither of us could utter a word; our eyes were silent. The mutual intention was clear, to make sweet love! Our bodies, lit with desire, penetrated each other, and our lips, hung with kisses, attached themselves and detached themselves with a spontaneous, irregular, and frequent intermittency. Shaky, confused hands caressed and took the innocence of our flesh with candor. The intensity of our gestures of love led us to a cry of joy. I rejoiced, sipping the purity of these moments until the last drop. Outside the tower it began to rain, and the dripping broke the spell that had wrapped us.

We remained embraced, observing through the little door the rain pressing on with ever increasing rhythm. After, I do not know how long, it finally stopped raining, offering us the chance to get out of the walls of the tower and savor the intrusive scent that emanated from the wet earth. Serenity returned. Our eyes, illuminated with new light, did not stop penetrating, like two crazy people in love. The words spoken did not help us; our bodies were talking to each other, and our figures in the trees looked like scarecrows under the sun, rain, and wind. So, full of love, we walked the path that led to the cottage. Here we gathered our things together and walked toward the station, promising to return to this wonderful place. The train pulled into the city, and although it was late, we went home to get rid of our wet clothes. Our naked bodies burned with desire. So, kiss after kiss we both lost track of time, ending up in bed making love. We were happy and aware that we had quenched the thirst for love in our throats and that all this had happened because we wanted it to happen.

Each morning of the next week, I took the van that on Monday Master Saverio's brother-in-law had parked by my house. The first day of driving was the most tragic, since I had to learn to drive again after a long time. The engine, in fact, often sobbed and consequently went out. The second day was better because I chose the wider side streets and this made me feel safer. Fifteen days later I was proud of myself for having acquired sufficient confidence in driving, and all without being next to the instructor.

I was in the shop regularly, and every time I delivered a console, a prie-dieu, a bedside table, Master Saverio collected the money from the various repairs, telling customers not to send other work because he was about to go on vacation. That was when I realized he could really pull this off. Mastro Saverio, in fact, had pulled a fast one. During the daylight hours I carried out my duties, while at night, from the exit that led into the atrium, Master Saverio was able to load the heaviest equipment on a truck without being noticed by anyone. The destination was outside the province, where he had found a buyer who bought a large part of all the work machines. Only good wooden planks remained in the room to be burned, and I did nothing.

Mastro Saverio kept his promises. He gave me the sum that we had agreed upon and the second keys of the van together with the title, the passbook, and the transfer of property that he himself had notarized. The first week of August vacation, the workers and the artisans put up posters saying "Closed for Holidays." Mastro Saverio, on the other hand, had posted the sign: "Closed for Mourning." We said goodbye to each other and good luck, and I haven't seen him since.

Maria Clara was waiting for me in the house while I tried to park the van in front of the door to make it less difficult to load stuff. Our goal was to spend the holidays going around Puglia. Along with food and clothes, we also carefully packed thirty paintings in the van. Our plan was to stop in the towns where they held the fairs and feasts of their patron saints. Before leaving, we passed by Lorenza's house, because she too was part of the adventure. Lorenza was already in hitchhiker mode, and seeing us, she signaled her presence. I slowed down, pulled over where I had to, and stopped. She had a short haircut, compared to the last time; she wore a bobbed hairstyle in the style of Valentina's fringe, the comic book character created by Guido Crepax.

I opened the tailgate, and she arranged the stuff. I closed the hatch and we both got on board where Maria Clara was waiting between us. The first stop was for gas, then onto the long strip of asphalt, singing happily as we ate up the kilometers.

Along the Adriatic, we often stopped to allow the van's engine to cool down and to stretch our legs. During one of the many stops, next to our van was another car which obviously had the same problems with its engine overheating. At the helm there were two people in their forties, a man and a woman. From what we understood, they were nice folk and easy to talk to.

They also were traveling the country, but they knew what they were doing. They were, in fact, peddlers of peanuts, olives, and dried fruit, who went to the patronal feasts of the country to sell their goods.

"Follow us; we'll take you to the town square where the festa takes place," they told us. I started the van and followed them, keeping a safe distance. Paying attention to the driving, I sometimes spoke with Maria Clara and Lorenza, telling them about the characteristics of these towns along the coast. They were places rich in saints and madonnas coming from the sea that were celebrated by the people with solemn ceremonies, setting up and decorating sacred trees and squares with magnificent lights. The festivities generally lasted three days, during which city and other bands performed concerts in the bandshell and then played behind the procession in honor of the saint. The lights were extinguished in the late evening, and the sky for a few minutes remained black and empty and then filled with explosions and colors of fireworks. On the last day, in the afternoon, the same sky swallowed colored balloons of various sizes. Finally, at night, the technicians began to dismantle all the lighting and the bandshell. The showmen loaded their rides on the trucks after having disassembled them and headed for other towns where saints and madonnas waited for them to start other parties.

Meanwhile, the couple's van stopped in the town square. It was a town in the hinterland where the lights were already mounted; on the fronds of the holm-oaks that adorned the square hung strings of multi-colored lights. A stretch of road divided the square into two unequal parts. The largest had a war memorial in the center; the smallest was occupied by a gas station and a newspaper shop. The entire square was surrounded by a paved road that ran around it and where the workers had set up the poles that held the frames for the lights. Here vans occupied the spaces that had been assigned to them. Our two acquaintances, while organizing their stand, suggested that we go to the local police station to obtain permission to display the paintings on public land. That done, we laid some on the ground and propped others against the wall of a whitewashed house. Once we set up the paintings, we stood watch. People strolled by in festive dress; some approached, more out of curiosity, others showed indifference, and it wasn't until the evening that we managed to sell a painting. The gentleman who bought it asked that on the back of the canvas I confirm its authenticity by affixing my signature, and since it was a gift for his girlfriend, he also dictated a dedication to be transcribed. At the end of the first day of the patronal feast, we collected the paintings and returned them to the van.

The next morning, we woke early, and we walked through the streets and alleyways of the old town. It was dirty and abandoned, and this led us to move to other areas. We ended up in the park among majestic trees and green hedges where there were two fountains, one of which was only ornamental, while the other gushed drinking water. A little farther on, there was a small room used as a bar with two staircases outside and an arcade at the top. At the center of the square, in front of the bar, was a laurel plant pruned to a spear point, which seemed to have pierced the sky. That green oasis, as guardians, had two doves at the lowest point of the wall, two eaglets on the columns of the main entrance, and two pairs of rabbits, one for the first side entrance, and the other for the second. All these sculptures were in stone, while one was a bust depicting a local philosopher in bronze. Maria Clara was enthusiastic about that park more than me and Lorenza, so much so that she told us: "I could set a beautiful love story here." We encouraged her, almost in chorus, and asked "Who would be the protagonists?"

"You two, certainly not," she added, and continuing, she said: "You do not have the natural features. Do you see these stone rabbits? Just around them could be the plot of the story of the eventual protagonists. With these children jumping up, playing with each other, and the lovers who are photographed sitting on one of them, why not let the protagonists interact in this segment of park? The idea fascinates me, and even though I now have little time at my disposal, I will write some in my notebook, of that you can be sure."

Back in the square, a young man was busy drawing something on the asphalt. He was a *madonnaro* and held a figurine in his hand, skillfully sketching the portrait of the Madonna on that spot. With discretion, we set ourselves to observe him as his work progressed. Both Maria Clara and Lorenza showed a keen interest in the art that was being created in front of them, so much so that they remained almost enraptured. Lorenza, moreover, seemed struck by the charm of the young man and his movements. Maria Clara, instead, looking at me, said: "Sebastiano, guess what? I found the protagonist of my story. No doubt I will soon find other characters to join the story, but right now my mind is still working on it."

The procession was already passing through the square, and the *madonnaro* stared with satisfaction at the work he had just completed being covered with lots of coins. Lorenza noticed this and took the opportunity to talk to him. Maria Clara and I, as the night before, returned to the paintings, hoping to sell them to someone.

The statue of the Madonna, carried by the devotees on duty, solemnly moved through the crowd. There were those in tears, those who begged, and those who through faith asked for intercessions or called for miracles for them or their relatives. They pleaded in low voices, and when the clerk held out the donation box, they deposited their offerings, receiving in return a holy figurine with a prayer on the back.

The procession passed over the square, and leaving Maria Clara in front of the paintings, I went first to the tobacconist for cigarettes, and then to the grocery to buy sandwiches and drinks. On my return, Lorenza kept company with Maria Clara telling her about the conversation exchanged with the *madonnaro*, who remained focused on his work, overseeing his day's gain.

"His name is Sergio, and he recently graduated from art school; he also plays guitar." I interrupted her and told her. "Yes it's true, I remember seeing a guitar case on the sidewalk next to his chalks and his things."

"He's a professional session man for recording groups. He prefers folk and blues and contemporary music."

People left for lunch, and as we munched the focaccia, Sergio joined us after gathering his things and the offerings. We ate together, talking and contemplating the paintings.

Meanwhile the sky was darkening, and suddenly it started raining out of nowhere. Surprised, we scrambled to get the paintings and take them safely to the van. Sergio, however, ran to his Madonna to protect it from the water with cellophane, otherwise the chalk drawing would be completely ruined. The storm lasted for about an hour, jeopardizing the festa and our potential earnings. After a break of a good half-hour that resulted in an apparent calm, the storm broke out again, forcing us into a mass escape accompanied by curses directed at the sky and its inhabitants, gods or saints. The wind that raged carried away Sergio's covering, and the rain whitened the colors of the sacred icon, so that it seemed like the negative of a photo. The three of us persuaded ourselves to leave our exhibiting, reluctantly accepting the whims of time. Sergio, in turn, had resigned himself not to redo the work, content with what he had already earned, so he invited Lorenza to take a walk with him. Maria Clara and I, not to get bored, walked toward the park where she did nothing but take notes in her journal.

On our return to the city center, Lorenza showed us the charcoal sketch Sergio had drawn on Bristol sheet paper. Compared to my self-taught technique, Sergio was an academic copyist, and he had mastered the techniques of the portraitist. Maria Clara and I complimented him, and in couples, we walked together through the village. The storm, by now, had erased the festa, and we wanted to leave. The van was surrounded by the vehicles of the other merchants, and was blocked, making it impossible to leave. At another round of rain, we managed only to open the door of our van and settle as best we could between the paintings and other things. We could see lightning and hear thunder through the windows, and here, we passed the time with Sergio playing guitar and singing songs.

At midnight, the orchestra performed *Bolero*. We left, joining the crowd at the bandshell.

The concert ended with a long ovation, and the band headed to the bus, instruments in hand, to travel to another town. Sergio hurried off and called out a goodbye as he got on the bus. Lorenza explained that he was friends with the concert master, and had been invited to join them in their travel to another feast in Calabria.

On Monday, the festa continued with those from nearby towns who had been busy on Sunday. We stayed on in hopes of selling more paintings. By the end, our patience was rewarded when someone from the festival committee bought two. Meanwhile, the local band performed the final concert, after which the lights went out and the street cleaners arrived to clean up. One of them asked where we were headed next, and I told him I had learned this was the last festa of the month, and that we were headed home.

By late evening we made it to Lorenza's house. She jumped out, and after saying goodbye to me, hugged Maria Clara and whispered something into her ear.

On the way home, Maria Clara seemed happy with the adventure of the last three days, and of the income obtained, and perhaps of the love that had blossomed between Sergio and Lorenza since the two had exchanged their addresses. Inside the house, under the effect of the radio playing "Black Time," Maria Clara let herself go in a frenetic dance. I stood and watched her; she unloaded all the accumulated tension, probably dancing to those rhythms freed her of all the stress of the festa. After a shower, we made love and fell asleep.

When I woke early the next morning, I couldn't tell if I was listening to the roar of my van's engine or a hamster spinning in my head. I opened my eyes to see Maria Clara, sitting at the table, writing.

"Good morning, love," I told her with such joy in my heart. Then I hugged her and kissed her, adding: "Go ahead, in the meantime I'll make you a coffee with the Moka, and when you want, we'll go down to the breakfast bar, and then we'll go for a stroll. Don't worry, my love, let's not be bitter about what happened because of our inexperience; in the future we'll just do the best we can."

"Are you really saying that?" answered Maria Clara.

"And what's more, we need to work harder to improve our skills. People are attracted to my paintings, in galleries and at the festivals, so that when winter comes, unlike ants, we will continue to work. In this way, we'll be ready to get back on the road for the next holidays. With eventual, and hopefully decent earnings, we will try to make a book with all your stories, and so my paintings and your book will transform the van into a gallery and a bookshop."

Maria Clara listened to me, as if her mind crossed a space-time portal, she was so wrapped up in silence, then suddenly she told me: "Your intentions are extraordinary, even better if they are successful. This will happen on the condition that we do not become an assembly line with the goal of increasing our productions at all costs. That would lead us to producing low quality art, which doesn't fit our style. We have seven months until March to produce without fooling around. In short, we must be spontaneous. We make love when we feel the need; we do not program our daily or weekly fucking, even monthly. By behaving in this way, love would turn into a stupid repetitive habit that would lead us to boredom and a burning disappointment. I write when I feel like it, and you just paint. Furthermore, between one thing and another, I will keep giving private lessons at Lorenza's house. We'll put our earnings in a common box, making ours a marriage of acts and not words on legal paper. You can place a few paintings with gallery owners. In one way or another time will pass. At the end of February, if anything, let's go to the abandoned estate. We'll track down the owner and, if possible we can rent it, and live there."

"Love, our work unites us," I said with happiness in my eyes. "I propose that Lorenza join us; in any case, let's ask her."

She smiled and said, "We'll probably spend autumn and winter, as it were, under house arrest."

She drank more coffee, and I did the same, forgetting about the breakfast and our wandering around the city. We stayed at home, had lunch, and in the evening, Maria Clara finished her notes and was ready to write. I began thinking of our new project, hypothesizing any negative developments and thinking about what good they could offer us.

The sounds of the typewriter brought me back to my work and some new thoughts that came to me while I was driving the van and looking at the landscape through my rear-view mirror. In addition to the original perspective of a tree, a house, a neighborhood, I could paint the reverse, thus gaining two paintings of the same subject. This idea came to me for the first time while I was driving the van and looking at the landscape from the rear-view mirror. Warmed up by this novelty, the next day I wanted to introduce myself to the gallery owner. He was not there, but one of my paintings stood out in his window.

The price posted on the frame was five times more than I had sold it for and the signature was no longer mine. He had fucked me over, and I swore never to sell again to any gallery owner. I remembered what Maria Clara suffered with her writing. Ironically, I too had been plagiarized.

At home, when I told her about my discovery, she was furious, because it reminded her of the mocking smile that the thief of her story had on his fucking face. In order to free ourselves from the wrath that had seized us, we made love and eventually returned quietly to realizing our future plans.

About a week after our adventure at the patronal feast, Lorenza let us know that after many letters and phone calls, she and Sergio were a couple. Meanwhile, summer gave way to autumn, and the latter to winter. At the first stirrings of spring, Maria Clara and I decided to return to the estate near the half-ruined tower with the van and ask with whom we needed to talk to rent it.

The place hadn't changed; still full of air, light, and lots of greenery. A farmer passed by, and we asked him to direct us to whom could rent the large abandoned estate. We were lucky, as the person who he introduced us to immediately accepted our requests, asking us to pay in advance the full amount of a year's rent. We agreed, and seven days later, at the crack of dawn, we began to clean the place up and take out the weeds that invaded the doors and windows. Then we whitewashed the walls with lime milk, and with toolbox in hand I began to repair the doors and windows, made unusable by neglect. In two days, the estate, at least for the time being, had become cozy. Back in the city, with the help of Lorenza, we emptied the attic, and we could now say that we had moved permanently.

In this new country house I painted and read books, while my girlfriend typed her stories. During our breaks, we cuddled. I wandered through the fields, between the ancient buildings and the dry-stone walls. Probably, if someone had observed me, they would have thought I had escaped from a madhouse. Of course, I did not look good.

At times, I went to town to sell some paintings, to meet our needs. Sometimes the framers bought my paintings, and I took advantage of them to supply me with brushes, canvases, and colors. Then I would pass by the newsstand, buying several things to read, and with these burdens I would return to the country when the sun turned at sunset.

Meanwhile, Maria Clara had completed her labors at the typewriter, and she told me she had written thirty-two stories.

One day, to thank Lorenza for the help we had at the time of the move, we headed to the city to visit her, and if possible, invite her to spend a few days with us. At her home, she was happy, letting us know she was awaiting the arrival of Sergio and his sister Marcella, who accompanied her brother because she wanted to meet us. Sergio, in fact, had told her about our chance friendship. We insisted, and she accepted, as long as we alerted the brother and sister who would be arriving by train. We added that if they accepted, they could stay with us on the estate. Lorenza agreed and together we went to the station, where the two stepped down from the train that had arrived a few minutes late.

After Sergio introduced us to his sister, we told him that we were going to our new home, and that we would be happy to accommodate them. Sergio and his sister, winking, accepted, and we left the station in the van, heading toward the countryside. During the journey between questions and answers and some laughter, we got to know Marcella better. She said she belonged, together with other women, to a feminist movement called Metropolitan Indians. This collective made propaganda using a mimeograph in its headquarters, where the members spent most of their free time. They confronted issues such as clandestine abortion, contraception, and planned initiatives and various protests, by demonstrating outside the diplomatic offices of the countries where the genital mutilation practice of infibulation was performed.

It was not long before sunset when we passed the columns of the estate, still in the dark because of a bureaucratic misunderstanding that still deprived us of electricity. To avoid this inconvenience, we were provided with oil lamps and some gas lanterns. At the end of dinner, at bedtime, we gladly offered our bedroom to Lorenza and Sergio, while the two of us with his sister arranged our sleeping bags. At breakfast, exchanging our opinions, Marcella took the chance to tell us that she was about to leave to go to the office, offering Maria Clara the opportunity to bring her writings to the attention of the movement. This could mean sponsorship by the feminist cultural association, but her presence would be necessary. She suggested that Maria Clara should leave with Sergio, Lorenza, and Marcella for the city. Maria Clara immediately accepted Marcella's invitation, showing her enthusiasm for the eventual publication of some of her works at the feminist level. I, however, while agreeing with her decision to leave with friends, felt a sense of bitterness, imagining my loneliness in the period of her absence. In the afternoon, I drove them to the village station near the estate, where they got on the train.

Maria Clara told me that on the bedside table I would find her last effort, adding that she hoped for a good outcome from the experience she was about to undertake with her friend. Finally, she advised me to have patience during her absence, albeit a short one which perhaps could benefit both of us. I thought about all this while returning to the estate, and as soon as I stepped into the bedroom, I headed for the bedside table. There was the manuscript Maria Clara had told me about, and since I had some time to kill, I rushed to read it.

In this fucked up world, little has changed. After Vietnam, the forgotten wars recorded by the work of official press reporters lie hidden somewhere only in the dust, and not in public opinion, which is informed by drops of truth, like those from alternative newspapers, in the sea of lies. I, in the guise of a reporter, digging into the habits and customs of the people as a counterpart, wanted to write this love story. Reluctantly, I leave you, I hope for a very short period. I hope that the epilogue of this story is good and will not make me return to being a Penelope who weaves the same tapestry. Enjoy the reading.

The Stone Rabbit

The local train of the Southeast Railways arrived at 5 p.m. It pulled into the tired little station. That April day was particularly important for one of the travelers. He opened the door the moment he was sure the train was completely stopped. He had long hair, a thick beard, and wore jeans, gym shoes, and a white Asian-style shirt. Instead of wearing an old Texan hat, dropped over his eyes, he wore a halo; he could certainly have been mistaken for a saint. Instead, he was just a very sad-looking man with black, crossed eyes.

He threw the sleeping bag over the long, narrow wall that separated the two sections of the railway and waited for the train to leave. In addition to the sleeping bag, the stranger carried a travel bag and a guitar case. Calm and oblivious to the looks that rained on him, the man crossed the tracks.

After a while, the water that came out of the fountain near the station satisfied his thirst and refreshed him. He continued along the tree-lined avenue that led to the village. He walked with a light step. It seemed to him that the water had given him energy, and much of his weariness disappeared.

The man at the newsstand explained to the stranger that he was wasting his time trying to find accommodation, since there were only a few days to go before the great country festival, and all the hotels were already filled. The stranger thanked him and left. He walked through the streets of the historical center, pausing from time to time to stop and look at the old white houses, which to his eyes looked like ghosts in dirty sheets.

The last rays of sunshine of that day posed as usual on the balconies at sunset. The women looked out and hurriedly went back to their laundry, the evening was now coming. There was a strong smell of basil and mint in the air. It seemed to him that every pore of his skin absorbed the joy that his lungs felt breathing in that air.

He walked along a downhill road. The high arch at the end marked the boundary of the old quarter, with elm trees scattered all over the place. In that space, the rides had been set up, and some were already in operation. The deafening music of the amplifiers bothered him, and he ended up leaving. He stopped in front of a restaurant, anticipating the chickens on the spit that were drawn on the sign. He reflected for a moment on the possibility of entering, and then, without hesitating again, walked inside.

The owner of the restaurant served him courteously. The man ate and drank, then paid and left. Along the way he remembered the questioning glances of the people in the restaurant, He knew well what they wanted to ask him and what they had thought of him, but he did not care, he had something else on his mind.

The technicians tested the lights, arranged on wooden arches painted in white, and others still arranged on top of the supporting poles, creating imaginative designs. On the gray tile bandstand, the orchestra had completed its concert.

He walked on toward the concourse, leaving behind the mesh of light bulbs. Meanwhile, he had arrived at the public park, composed of a lower part and an upper part, and there he decided on the latter. On either side of the entrance there were two columns, and on each one of its claws stood an eagle in stone, sculpted by no one he knew, one whose beak faced north, the other south. The man crossed the gate and, with a determined step, went to a round piazza filled with palm trees surrounded by flowers. He sat on an edge and looked at the stone rabbits at the end of the walkway near a granite bench.

Intent on turning the memories upside down, to distract himself, he pulled out the guitar. He adjusted the strings and managed to tune it well. With a deep and melancholy voice, he sang old songs. The wind ruffled his hair and froze his hands, but he continued to sing, keeping his eyes fixed on the stone rabbit. That sculpture, for him, contained an existential secret.

He couldn't hold back the tears. Suddenly, he stopped playing and cried. He ran to the rabbit and knelt down before it. He caressed and hugged it, kissing the hard stone, while the tears ran down his cheeks, lost in his beard. He pulled back, stood up, and went away sobbing. He kept wandering through the flowerbeds, stopping from time to time. The opaque lights of the street lamps created a surrealist image that spoke with shadows.

He crossed the street and went into the lower park. He went down the steps, walking under young fir trees, looking for space to spread his sleeping bag. He found a small spot of grass, stretched out, and looked at the stars that were scattered among the branches. Then he zipped the bag up to his eyes and fell asleep.

Along the main avenue, little girls dressed in white walked in rows of three. They were elementary school students. Given the good weather of April, their teacher had taken them out. At the center of the square, the girls broke out of formation and ran off to play, attracted to the sounds of the guitar and the man singing. The bravest ones stepped forward and by the man's gesture of invitation they began to approach, after getting an OK from their teacher.

"Can you sing a song?" asked the girls.

"Do you know the song The house in Via dei Matti number zero?" *replied the man.*

"Yes," they shouted in chorus.

"Then we'll sing it together: "There was a very nice house, without attic without kitchen ...*"*

Together, all the girls continued to sing. At the end of the cheerful song, the young teacher asked the stranger if he knew any other song that spoke of love. The man told her that he only knew old songs.

"Okay" the teacher nodded, "then play what you like."

With that, he started singing.

"With this face of a foreigner,/ I'm just a real man even if it doesn't seem so to you ...*"*

As he continued to sing, his voice came out more and more uncertain, however he completed the performance of the song.

"We know this song," said two little girls who for their likeness were certainly twins.

"That's funny; it's a very old song," said the man.

"We have that old record at home," the two little girls added, "and sometimes it skips. We know that song by heart."

The man lovingly repeated the initial chords and the girls began to sing. They did it so well that they earned the applause of everyone present. At the end of the applause, the students got ready to leave, while the teacher and the man introduced themselves.

"My name is Anna Costa," said the girl.

"I am Gabriele De Angelis" replied the man, who added: "Among the many things I have done, I have also managed to find the time to scribble down a thing or two."

The "House of the Geraniums" was the largest and most important hotel in the area. Gabriel went there in the afternoon. It was a large house, painted red and with a sloping roof, like Swiss houses. At the main entrance there were huge white stone columns. To enter it, you had to go through a small shady garden, with a majestic fir tree planted a long time ago. He rang the bell and waited. He looked at that unusual house and thought to himself: "What a place!"

The owner invited him in, just to keep him from standing on the sidewalk. They both stood in the narrow path covered with wild grass. The owner with a kind voice told him:

"If it is your intention to stay for a long time, I would advise you to come back in a few days. Now the hotel is full. After the festa many rooms will be free, if you can be patient for a few more days ... "

Gabriele looked at her with serene eyes and, without saying anything else, left.

The following Saturday evening the square was teeming with people all dressed up, walking up the main street leading to the piazza. On the sides, under the lights, stalls stood selling American peanuts, colored balloons, and toys of all kinds. Everyone was waiting for the procession along the sidewalks. Gabriele, who had a regular permit, chose a paved area on a street corner out of the procession's way. He borrowed a broom from the nearby barber, swept more than three yards of road, and carefully drew a large rectangle. He opened his wallet and pulled out a holy figurine of the Madonna whose festa was being celebrated.

In less than twenty minutes he had sketched the figure with a white chalk. He pulled out colored chalk carefully arranged in a small cardboard box and began to color the tiles. First with the strongest colors, then with the soft colors, and finally, he added details. Before the work was completed, coins were raining on the portrait of the Madonna. When Gabriele had finished his work, he returned the chalks, cleaned his hands, and went to sit on the steps of the church.

The procession passed, but Gabriele's eyes were absent. His catatonic demeanor clashed with those of the people, full of emotions that could be read in all the corners of their eyes and excited expressions. The procession continued its path, interspersed with short stops, according to traditon. At the end of it all, two musical bands followed the procession, alternating sacred and popular marches. Gabriele picked up the coins in the picture and left. He returned to the park of young firs, slipped into the warm sleeping bag, and sank into sleep.

In the morning, when he woke, he took his things and headed for the upper side of the villa. He went to sit on one of the four stools surrounding a round table, with his elbows resting on a plane inlaid with black and white pieces, a simple reproduction of a chess game. In front of his eyes, fifty paces away, the stone rabbit seemed to come out to cross the narrow avenue. Instead ... it stood there motionless, nailed to the asphalt to act as a guardian along with its twin that at that moment, given the position

of Gabriele, remained hidden behind the low hedge. The singing of the
birds that jumped among the branches of pines and firs awakened him.

All the thoughts that occupied his head emerged, and Gabriele began to
examine them. First: He was not a stranger; the fact that he made himself
pass for such had a very specific purpose. Second: His intentions were clear
enough; he was looking for someone and the discovery was important to
him because she knew everything about his past. However, his eyes tried
to hide his past. For a moment he rubbed them and seemed to come out
of a dream. What he saw challenged his intentions.

The twin girls who had sung with him descended the steps of the
chalet in slow motion in the company of a young woman. He thought
that the woman was their teacher and realized when he saw that the
female figure was the person he was looking for. There she was, walking
with a light and sure step. The twins preceded her by a couple of meters
before they got ready to jump on one of the two stone bunnies. The young
woman stood and watched them closely. Her light brown eyes filled
with tears, and she turned to hide them from the girls; as she did, she
noticed the man next to the lady. Her thoughts moved in his direction,
and soon her feet followed.

She approached him with a sense of fear, but the man showed no
interest, absorbed as he was in playing his game. He had arranged pine
nuts on the side with the white squares and small stones on the black
squares on the other. In reality, he pretended to play, because the woman's
approach had unnerved him. Then he looked up and greeted her with his
hand. The woman bowed her head in greeting. She had wonderful eyes,
and at the same time, seemed sad. For her part the woman felt horrified,
or perhaps it was only the man's black, cross-eyed eyes that conveyed the
restlessness that stirred her.

After a long silence, he said: "You know? I expect from you the usual
question that everyone asks me."

"Are you a stranger?" The woman replied dryly.

"Exactly, this was the question I was waiting for. No, I'm not a stranger.
I was born in this country, I'm a writer, which is why I'm always around."

The woman, unsatisfied, resumed asking: "You've been gone from
here for a while?"

"Yes, for several years."

"I'm trying to remember if I've met you or not,"

"Go ahead," said the man, "sometimes it's good to fantasize about your past."

"No," replied the woman after thinking a little, and then she said: "You remind me of someone, but that someone can't be you."

"Who was he?" the man asked her gently.

"All right! I have no reason to hide it from you. You remind me of my girls' father. You can see them there, on the rabbit, the same one where their father and I played together when we were kids. Then he died, and it was a shame; soon after his death the girls were born."

So saying, the woman closed her eyes and fell silent. The man, embarrassed, spoke again. "I am a writer, and I seem to have told you already. What you told me, however, can only be part of his life, and if you like, you can tell me the rest."

Meanwhile the twins were running toward their mother, and when all three of them met side by side, they introduced themselves. The young woman was named Marta Macerasa, and her girls were Flora and Laura, and both had the mother's last name. After getting acquainted, Marta, very gracefully, managed to get Flora and Laura back to their games. Then, settling down with elegance on the other stool, with a touch of emotion, she began to narrate her misadventures.

"Ermanno La Cupa was my boyfriend; he was fourteen; I was thirteen. His eyes were a pure blue, and his hair was brushed brown. His parents died, and he lived in a hospice together with old folks. We attended the same school, but we were in different classrooms; he was in the third grade and I the second. We knew each other as children, and since then we promised ourselves that we'd get married when we were old enough and then we would be together forever.

"We often came to this park, and he enjoyed making fun of a bronze bust at the other entrance. The stone rabbit, then, was our faithful playmate. One day we decided not to go to school. The school's gossips spilled everything they knew about our relationship. When this all came to my father's ear, blinded by anger, he ran toward us swinging his fists and later forbade us to be together. We did not see each other for two weeks, and both Ermanno and I began to get sick. That's when the deceptions began. And again, we got caught and all hell broke loose! My father threatened me by telling me

that if I wouldn't leave Ermanno, he wouldn't allow me to attend school anymore. Unfortunately, I had to go along with it even though I didn't want to. For two months, I did not talk to Ermanno anymore. I seemed to be going crazy. That childish infatuation was becoming serious, and even though I did not speak to him, I knew that he suffered as well.

"In March, I had my first menstruation. I wanted to tell Ermanno about my joy of becoming a young lady, and I did so by sending him a note through a trusted friend. After a few days the same person sent me the answer. He was happy that I had become a young lady, but it was very sad because we had not been able to talk to each other for a long time, and we just had to settle for furtive glances in the school's courtyard. My father accompanied me in the morning, and my mother came to pick me up. In short, I was facing a real ordeal. Day after day, everything that concerned us proceeded badly and ended worse. He secretly followed me, just to get a glimpse. My parents, in addition to the role of guard dogs, always reproached me and in any case, I was forced into silence, suffering the pain of being so, until one day ...!

"It was end of the school year. They were fighting in Ermanno's classroom. The noise and the screams could be heard inside our class. Then, suddenly, everything was silent. A few minutes later, I went out, to go to the bathroom, and I saw Ermanno in the corridor, standing, with tears in his eyes. He looked out of the window. I realized that he had been the cause of all that disturbance and, as a result, had been punished by being sent outside the classroom. He noticed me and I motioned for him to follow me, and I entered the bathroom, certain that he would soon be there. Ermanno arrived, in silence, closed the door behind him and threw his arms around my neck. He began to kiss me, and with his hands caressed me. I understood that we would go further, and so it was. Moments passed, or maybe minutes, and the inevitable happened. We made love, and for both of us it was the first time. Then...!

"I pulled myself together and slinked down the hallway, waiting for the red to disappear from my cheeks and, after a while, I returned to the classroom. A few days later the school year ended. For Ermanno, however, school continued, as he had to take the eighth-grade exams. For me, however, school, at least for that year, was finished. On my birthday Ermanno took the exams. My friends came home to greet me with gifts *and, among them was a 45-round disc titled "Lo Straniero" by Georges Moustakì, with a dedication on the cover that said: "To the greatest love of my existence, with affection. Ermanno." I hid the cover in my diary and played that record over and over.*

"Later, I learned that the school year for Ermanno had ended positively. He was among those promoted, and I was happy, although in my heart I felt that I would never see him again. My father, in fact, had planned that I would do my last year in a private school because, according to him, that was the only way I could chase Ermanno from my head.

"'You have to become someone,' he told me, and again. 'You must marry a man who has titles, not a starving man.'

"Away from prying eyes, during a meeting with Ermanno, I told him everything. He clearly did not agree with what my father had decided for me. I was not happy with that decision either, but I was too afraid to go against my father. Ermanno, for his part, while feeling the same sense of fear, wanted to take the risk of facing him and did not lose heart.

"On the last Sunday of June, we had been invited to a first communion lunch. In the morning we went to the church to attend the ceremony. At the celebration, we took pictures with relatives, and finally we all went to a restaurant by the sea. After lunch, we went out for a walk. I noticed Ermanno coming toward us from the top of the road. He had pedaled his bicycle more than twenty kilometers to talk with my parents. Stopping, he got offf the bicycle and, after leaning it against the wall, came up and asked to talk to my father. My father indulged him, even though he seemed displeased with his presence. They went away on the cliff and spoke, so I could not hear what was said. I could watch the two discussing, but from where I was, I could only see their gestures. At a certain point, I realized that words passed to actions because of the intensity with which they moved against each other. My father, in fact, threw himself at Ermanno and beat him up, but there was no reaction on Ermanno's part. I ran to them to be able to understand more, and I noticed my father was quite angry and was offending Ermanno, scorning his poverty. Ermanno, in tears, said that it was not right the way he was treated and that his poverty had nothing to do with anything, because he had good intentions to learn a trade that would allow him to earn a living. He wanted, however, the consent of my father so that we could continue to see each other.

"'Not even in your dreams,' cried my father, who added: 'You, if you have not yet understood, must leave my daughter alone. She's not for you. I advise you to stay away from her. Try to find the right partner among your peers.'

"Ermanno turned to me and said, 'What do you think about all this?'

"My father looked at me and scared me, in fact I couldn't respond.

"'I'm talking to you, Marta,' Ermanno continued, 'and if you do not want me anymore, tell me it's you and not your father.'

"I persisted in my silence, and he went back to saying that he needed me and that, if I no longer loved him, he no longer had a reason for living. I did not even have time to say anything; my father chased me, and as I walked away, I heard Ermanno shouting at me: 'Don't you want to keep loving me? Then I swear to you that I will kill myself.'

"In a fit of madness, he rushed down from the rocks and ran along the beach where the first swimmers enjoyed the afternoon sun. He ran, and completely undressing jumped into the water, slamming against the rush of the waves. Abandoning himself, every time the sea passed over his body, in a few moments as he disappeared from the sight of those present. I remained motionless, shocked and incredulous, but in my heart, I was hoping he would suddenly emerge. Later, on the shore, they found only the clothes he had been wearing and no trace of his body.

"The police were alerted and soon arrived with the special divers team. A search began that lasted until late evening and then resumed the following day without results. There was no trace of Ermanno. The investigations went on. They lasted more or less for two more days, then, he was given up as missing. During all this waiting, I was a wreck and felt a strong sense of guilt that did nothing but increase the hatred of my father for having caused that terrible episode. A few weeks later, everything was silenced. After all, what had the town lost? Only a starving boy, a misfit and nothing else, except me, no one else shed tears over Ermanno's disappearance.

"A month later I missed my period, but I did not worry about it much; I blamed all this on strained nerves and the tension that accumulated during those terrible days. Sometime later, without thinking of it, I went to the doctor for my checkup. The results came, and the doctors told me that I was pregnant. I was shocked. I asked myself how I could find the *courage tell this to my family. I waited a few days hoping that everything would change, but it was useless. As a result, though frightened, I told everything to my mother. At first, she said nothing, but then, when she told my father, I began to tremble. I was angry and afraid that they were going to kill me. They did not. I believe because they were overwhelmed by doubt about how they had behaved with Ermanno; my hopes of ever seeing him again were dying. In their behavior I read a sincere concern that they were worried for my health, considering the state in which I found myself, where I risked a trauma even worse than what I was now facing. Day after day I saw their attitude toward me change, aware of what I was carrying in my womb. Meanwhile, my belly grew, and my parents did not fail to be near me. Finally, I went to the hospital and waited impatiently for the fruit of that stealthy relationship to be born.*

"Two twin girls were born. Their eyes were blue, similar to those of Ermanno. I cried a lot that day, but I wished that the father of the two baby girls was weeping with me the same tears of joy that I had for the results of our love. Ermanno, however, was not there, he was dead, and this certainty did nothing but prolong my tears. Leaving the hospital, I went back to my parents' house, and I was constantly thinking about my becoming a woman, a mother, and a widow without ever having been a child.

"The little ones were baptized by my father and my mother, and I called them Flora and Laura, giving them my last name. Since then I have been taking care of all that was necessary for their good. Ever since they took their first steps, I have brought them to this park, where the stone rabbit was; this is what amuses them most. Often they ask to listen to the record that Ermanno gave me, and whenever I place it on the turntable they behave as if they are performing a ritual. Eight years have passed since then, and they issued a certificate of death, since his body had not yet been found. I asked to get a plot at the cemetery. I was given one and I had a marble cross planted with Ermanno's age engraved upon it: Fourteen Years. Every Sunday, I went to visit that tomb, and more often than not, I also took the girls."

The story told by Marta lasted for more than half an hour. Gabriele had listened in silence, without interrupting her. At last he felt the need to speak, and without hesitating, he said: "Can I tell you something?"

"Of course," she replied, hiding her embarrassment.

"Yours is a very sad story. In fact, what you have suffered can be noticed from a distance; you can read it on your face, and even if I wanted to write a story like this, I couldn't."

Marta jumped up, shaken by Gabriele's words, and a little nervous, said, "Don't try to write something like this. I told you everything, just to let off steam. It is now water under the bridge, and it makes no sense to turn it into fiction."

Gabriele looked her in the eye and noticed two big tears dripping down her cheeks.

"Don't worry," he said, "I won't write anything like that."

After a handshake, Marta reassured herself, grabbed her daughters, and led them away. Gabriele took out the guitar and began to play and followed them out of the corner of his eye.

The school near the park is a huge stone building with windows and arches that embellish the entrance. All around there is an immense space outlined by green pines, and the main road crosses the upper part of the school where the main gate is. Gabriele gazed through the link fence at the children who were lined up, accompanied by their teachers. After the sound of the bell and the greeting of the teachers, the rows of schoolchildren melted, and here and there they ran joyfully through the courtyard. There were those who chased each other, one threw the notebook of his companion in the air, and another started kicking a soccer ball.

The teacher, Anna Costa, went out together with some colleagues from the main gate where the children were having fun and recognized Gabriele a little further on. She left the group to meet him.

"Hi, Gabriele, how are you?"

"Fine, thanks."

"Did you find a place to stay?"

"Yes, since last night I've been at the House of Geraniums, in an old stable, quite comfortable as a guesthouse."

"I'm glad," said Anna who asked, "You have a reason to stay here?"

"It's simple," said Gabriel, "I was born here."

"Your relatives? I mean, don't you have any relatives who can put you up?"

"No! Some are dead, and others have emigrated to other countries."

"Excuse me, but why aren't you married?"

"Why should I get married? I lead this solitary life, and that's fine with me. Should I force a woman to follow me? Surely, she would soon get tired of me, and of this gypsy life I lead. Mine was a personal choice, but I can assure you that, despite being aware of it, I can't travel with full boxes."

"Now I have to leave you," said the teacher, "my boyfriend is waiting for me."

Across the street was a parked white Giulia T Alfa Romeo and a young man dressed elegantly, waiting impatiently.

"Goodbye, Gabriele, see you again."

Anna ran to the car. Meanwhile, the young man started the engine, and as soon she closed the door, the car left.

"Who is that guy?" The young man said to his girlfriend.

"He's a writer, I met him in the park while I was taking the children out to play. He was there with a guitar and his things, and the children were attracted to the music, so we all got to have a conversation with him. I would have told you before if I thought you cared. You, however, as always, have your head elsewhere. So, are you still intent on marrying the widow? "

"Yes, because Marta will give me what you can never give me."

"So why do you keep coming to me?"

"Simple, you give me what she has not yet given me."

"You disgust me. You're a brutal and abominable being, how did I fall in love with a guy like you?" Anna frowned. Rocco, as the young man was called, went on diverting the conversation with great ease.

"Do you want to be a drifter?" Rocco said almost provoking her, and with malice added: "It fits you comfortably. You've got the experience. Do it, I'm not jealous. Careful though, he's crazy; all the artists are."

"What bullshit!" Anna replied, annoyed by the provocation, and then said, "I'm not a slut! I give you everything because I still love you, despite what you do to me. What do you think? You go around hunting for all the girls from neighboring towns, and do you think I'm so foolish that I don't know?"

Meanwhile they had come to a pine forest adjacent to a rural school, almost in open country. They got out of the car and started walking on the soft pine needles, continuing to exchange sharp opinions.

"Listen," said Rocco, "I came to get you because today I want you. Forget about all of this and give me a kiss."

Anna threw herself into his neck, kissing it ardently. After all, she wanted to make love with that handsome young man. Afterward, however, there remained a bitter taste in her mouth and a great emptiness in her soul, and then returned the remorse and the rancor that pushed her to hate him.

Marta was busy cleaning; the twins were in their room doing their homework. The grandparents, in turn, were away on a pilgrimage to Lourdes in France, planned by the local church parish. Marta continued her housework until she heard shouting in the children's room. She crossed the hallway and entered the room, where she thought the girls were arguing with each other. She asked why they were fighting; the twins had accused each other of copying their homework. The mother insisted, and raising her voice, asked them what it was.

"A composition assignment," they both answered in chorus, as if each had only been one to have opened her mouth.

"So. what's it about?" asked their mother with curiosity.

"Read it all, if you want," said the girls. So saying, they put both notebooks in Marta's hands. Above it, in large letters, was written: "Tell the impressions you had during the walk in the park."

She read both of their essays and realized that they were actually the same; they differed only in some grammatical errors. In practice, they had both the same impressions along the same lines of thinking.

Flora wrote: "I felt something magical in the air. The voice of man penetrated my little heart with great sweetness. I knew that song, but not sung that way, no! It was more true. Although sung like a lament, it was beautiful, and for a moment I thought that man could very well be my dad. From what our mother has always told us, Dad had blue eyes, those of the man who was singing were black. Our teacher devoured him with her eyes, even if she tried to hide it, but I, in particular, noticed the way she looked at him. The man, who was called Gabriele, was staring at the stone rabbit, where Laura and I were sitting. I was very sad to think that a stranger would make a memory that did not belong to him, because my parents already played as children on these rabbits and on the other two located next to the bar in the park. We told him that we knew 'The Stranger,' and we sang the song together again, but that time he really put *his heart into it. In my opinion, he was a musician. The teacher, however, told us that he was a writer. I think that man, when he will leave from our country, will become a legend, the legend of St. Gabriele."*

Laura's theme was identical, and she noted the same sensations, the same details, and even wrote: "That man could very well be my father."

Marta remained silent, dumbfounded by what she read, and pondering it she also found several similarities between Gabriele and Ermanno. She tried to reassure the girls by telling them that there was nothing wrong if each one had written the theme with more or less similar words. It was probably because they were twins that they had the same impressions. In principle, they would have received the same grade. Not worrying too much, Marta went up on the terrace to spread the laundry on the line, and thinking about what happened before, she asked herself, "Damn it, why did these memories have to surface right now? Is it possible that I must continue to suffer, and right now, that I have decided to marry? Ermanno is dead, and the rest doesn't matter." It was not true. Marta still remained tied to Ermanno, for her it was the only true, unforgettable love, and if that writer resembled him, she could not but detest him.

The owner of the hotel knocked at the front door, number eleven. Gabriel opened and asked what she wanted. The lady replied that there was a visitor for him and that, since it was a woman, according to the agreements, she could not lead her up to the room. In any case, out of hospitality, she had made her sit in the salon. Gabriele thanked her and begged her to wait patiently for a few minutes, just enough time to get cleaned up. Sitting on a sofa, Anna Costa killed time by solving crossword puzzles. Gabriele appeared before her. She dropped the puzzle of the magazine and turned her attention to him. She got up and went to greet him, inviting him to take a walk outside the hotel. Gabriele immediately accepted. After taking a coffee offered by the lady owner, they left the building. It was less than an hour before noon, and the two walked among the avenues of the Young Firs park, chatting with some seriousness. During these conversations Anna began to tell him a story.

It was Rocco, her infamous boyfriend of that morning at school, who flirted with her and at the same time was doing what he could to be able to marry Marta. The latter, in turn, had been confiding to her that since she had met Gabriele, she had entered into a crisis. Anna claimed that Rocco had made Marta believe that he was a childhood friend of Ermanno and that, after his death, the idea of wanting to marry her had come to him. In reality, Rocco was pretending to play the part of his friend, not because of what he had said, but because Marta was rich. Being a born tramp, Rocco thought of combining business with pleasure. Marta had only partially accepted him at least in the beginning, and through his suffocating insistence that he knew many different ways to persuade people, women in particular. Then she said yes to his marriage requests. Anna went on, "And since then I began to risk being the fifth wheel, at least until they were at the altar. You know, and he insisted; I read the theme that the students had done at home about the walk to the park, and the twins associated your figure with that of their father. The mother, afraid that something was wrong with her children, came to me to air her concerns. I ask you, therefore, and indeed I beg you, not to enter into this story, so as not to further torment that poor thing."

Gabriele, in turn, told her that he knew Rocco. Less than a year younger than him, between the past and the present he had not changed at all in his character and his ways of treating people. Rocco was a narcissist, full of vanity par excellence, and fake from head to toe. What he did not understand, however, were the feelings of the two women toward such a bum and who, even knowing his intentions, accepted his courting. Anna explained to him that she was hopelessly in love and that she hoped until the last moment that he would give up on the idea of marrying Marta.

Marta wanted him more than anything else to be a father to the girls, and although Rocco could not be that ideal father imagined by mother and daughters, good or bad, at least they would have had someone on their side. Gabriele promised her that he would talk to Rocco and reason with him. He accompanied Anna to the village and, after saying goodbye, concentrated on what he was about to do by dealing with all the possible outcomes.

The pool hall was teeming with people at the tables. Inside, there were only young people, and each was completely immersed in his favorite game. Gabriele asked the manager if by chance he knew Rocco. He raised his hand and pointed his finger at four young men playing billiards.

"There, that well-dressed guy is Rocco. However, I do not know if it is wise to disturb the game," the manager said, "He goes crazy if anyone bothers him while he's playing."

The last sentences of the manager did not intimidate Gabriele who slowly and as if nothing had happened headed for the table. Rocco maneuvered the cue with great skill, especially when he was beating his the opponents, attracting everyone's attention.

"Are you Rocco?" Gabriele said in a defiant tone.

"Yes," replied Rocco, without even looking to see who had asked him.

"I would like to have a chat with you if you can, and if you do not mind, I would like to play."

Rocco smiled. With a mocking and defiant air, he turned to that brave patron and said:

"After this game, I still have three more to play. We'll talk about it in a couple of hours. Didn't anyone teach you that before talking you should introduce yourself?"

"You're absolutely right," said Gabriele who then introduced himself. Rocco was surprised by the personality shown by this man and, a little annoyed, refused the hand that Gabriel extended to him as a sign of respect and added, "Now, don't mess with me. We'll see each other in two hours, as I said before, and like it or not, get away from here, before my nerves get the best of me."

Gabriele did not move an inch. Then Rocco raised his voice, "Don't you understand? You're bothering me. Get out of here."

Having had his say, he continued to play, pretending nothing had happened. While Rocco was aiming the cue, Gabriele grabbed his arm, took the cue out of his hands, and said, "I have two things to tell you; either you stop this game and follow me, or I take you out of here myself."

Rocco reacted instinctively and took a swing at Gabriele with the back of his hand. He missed. Gabriele not only managed to dodge the blow but, whirling around, grabbed Rocco by the collar of his jacket, kicked his ass, and lead him, passing through a crowd of stunned onlookers, out of the pool hall. Outside, an embarrassed Rocco got cocky. "So tell me! Why are you so interested in talking to me?"

Gabriele looked him straight in the eyes.

"First, you have no business marrying Marta. You're doing it only for the money. Why are you pretending to be Ermanno's friend? You've never been a friend of his. If you were, you wouldn't have misled her. In fact, you would have done anything to help her. Now what do you have to say?"

"Excuse me," Rocco replied, almost disoriented by the words he had heard, "what have you got to do in this story? Do you always get caught up in things that do not concern you?"

"They concern me, all right," added Gabriele, "and I prefer to answer this question later." Insisting, he added: "Let's get back to us. Second point. What is Anna to you? You do nothing but delude her and run after her whenever you feel the need. Will you do the same even after you marry Marta? Mark my words. You will not marry her!"

"Who's going to stop me? You?"

"Yes, me," Gabriele said, showing his teeth, and then said, "Now I'll explain what I'm doing in this story. Many years ago you were a greedy and mischievous boy and, when Ermanno flirted with Marta, it was you who spied on her and told her father and the teachers of the school about it. You were envious of the happiness of those two kids and told a lot of lies just to put Ermanno in a bad light, the boy whom you said was your friend. You stood on the sidelines when he died. Then you even thought of claiming a friendship that has never been there, and day by day you drew Marta closer to you. Later you met Anna, and you could not help but delude her too, not giving up the ambitions you had for Marta. Listen to me well, the girls need a real father and a lot of affection, not false promises like yours; if you marry Marta, you'll end up ruining them too."

"Who are you to talk to me this way?"

"I am Ermanno."

"What are you talking about?" Rocco blurted out, "Ermanno died a long time ago, and if he's still alive, as far as I can see, he certainly can't be you."

"Don't worry. I'll set you straight soon enough. Right now I'm telling you for the last time, don't marry Marta! If you do, something will bury your illusions."

"Everything is already decided. We'll get married by the end of June, and neither you, nor Anna, will do anything to stop me."

June passed quickly. Every document concerning marriage had been carefully prepared with care, every aspect taken into consideration down to the smallest detail, everything was in perfect order. The last Saturday of the month was the one set for the wedding, which was also the same day as the twins' first Communion.

Friday night Marta had a nightmare. It was after midnight, it was hot, and she rolled under the sheets, anguish throbbing inside her wounded heart. She opened her eyes, and the darkness cleared. The nightmare began to assault her:

You could tell the house would collapse at any moment. The old house was crumbling, slapped by the north wind, with weeds clinging to what was left of the roof, and mortar cracking between the stones. In spite of this, she remained steadfast, and kept looking at the huge square at the foot of the cathedral that faced it. The many seasons it boasted, year after year, charged the humidity that increased the growth of the moss around the balconies and the hinges that barely held the glassless windows. An old lady came down the stairs. With caution she moved in slow steps. Her feet, in ragged slippers, sank in the dirt accumulated on the steps. She wore a black dress, and a handkerchief over her head covered most of her face. She slipped quietly from the doorway and allowed herself a brief pause by leaning her back against the wall for a few minutes. After a little breath, she opened the door of a basement, unleashing a deafening creak, as the hinges were rusty. She calmly went down, and to avoid tripping she left the door half-opened, just enough to make sure that at least one glimmer of light could pierce it. In the meantime, the sacristan finished arranging all the decorations and stood outside, in front of the great doorway, observing the shabby house before him, and said to himself, "Do you want to watch the old lady release them?"

As soon as he had finished speaking these words, there was a great flapping of wings accompanied by an incessant cooing coming from the cellar, and from the darkness of the half-open door peeked some beautiful white doves, like the snow. The lady's dogs, locked in a room on the first floor, began to bark. The old woman, now accustomed to the sudden barking of her animals, even though she was still in the basement, silenced them by yelling over their barking. Then she tossed a little corn here and there for the doves, who fluttered outside, lingering on the square as she went up the stairs.

Meanwhile, outside, the sacristan thought perhaps it would be better to warn the old lady to tell her to bring the doves back in. Soon the cars of the guests and, finally, the car of the couple, would arrive on the spot. If everything went well, it generally took a quarter of an hour, and this scene was repeated every day, but this time everything was done in advance by the order of the same sacristan, as the participants at the wedding had arrived early. Then finally the bride came, got out of a luxurious car, and headed for the entrance to the church, preceded by the twins. All three were dressed in white, each carrying a rose, followed by relatives and friends. At the altar, Rocco waited for Marta, trying to look serious, but inside he laughed and calculated that, a few seconds more, and the trap would be sprung.

Anna Costa finally entered and settled in near the main door of the church. She witnessed the ceremony, dazed by what was about to happen, fearing that at any moment she would start screaming and shouting. She restrained herself and resumed following the Mass that now saw the little girls receive the sacrament of the first Communion, and then passed to the bride and groom until they both pronounced the fateful "yes" to be husband and wife. Soon it was done. Anna did not break down, in her heart she felt a great desire to cry, but she did not give in. The sound of the organ filled the church. Anna looked up, as did Marta and the little girls, and they looked at the pipes of the organ which gave off columns of white smoke, like snow. In that bank of fog paper planes fluttered, and Marta grabbed one that had the colors of the rainbow on its wings. She flipped it, and inside appeared a rabbit drawn with a pen. At that very moment the wedding march was transformed. From a strange voice came a song only perceptible to Marta, and his last words were: "You will be queen and reign ..."

At that point, Marta woke up with a jolt dripping with sweat. It could not be true that she betrayed Ermanno to marry Rocco. The morning designated as the wedding date, still shaking, she dressed the children to go to the cemetery. She felt the need to go and pray at Ermanno's tomb, to get rid of that nightmare. She usually walked there, but this time she wanted to go by car to get there as fast as she could. She wanted first to pay homage to Ermanno and then go up to the altar.

The cemetery on the hill surrounded by cypresses was immersed in a sacred silence. The mother and her two daughters walked along the narrow street; the sky faded, the wind snarled among the leaves, and the first drops of rain began to fall. Marta looked up and had the impression that the sky was resting on the top of the cypresses. She decided to speed up her pace, clenching the rose in her teeth, and grabbed Flora and Laura by the hands: all three started running. The wind stopped. The rain came down heavily. They ran until they reached the little piece of land where the poor were buried. There was a man near Ermanno's tomb, and, though he was behind them, she recognized him immediately. It was Gabriele, the writer, who stood still and his clothes soaked. Marta shouted to him, "It's not right. You have no reason to come here. Leave the dead in peace! Your presence here disturbs the soul of those who do not belong to you. You have no right to be here. Get out. Get out! By behaving like that, violating the sensibilities of others, their feelings, their things, and for you, it's as if there's nothing wrong with all this. What do you know about pain? This pain of ours is sacred and you must respect it."

"I respect your pain," Gabriele answered in a soft and heartening voice, then he turned abruptly before the woman and the children, and keeping his head down said: "I was just leaving. But I wanted to see you for the last time, so I waited for you, because I hoped you would come."

Slowly and carefully, he raised his head! He wept, sobbed, and his eyes were no longer black and cross-eyed. Now in those pupils a marvelous celestial blue appeared; they were Ermanno's eyes!

"It's not possible!" Marta exclaimed when she realized what was happening.

"I'm Ermanno. I never died. I'm grew tired of being on the sidelines. Forgive me, and absolve me, Marta! I did everything wrong, unfortunately I did not know I had children, but now I'm no longer a frightened rabbit."

Marta, surprised, couldn't tell if the tears she shed were for the joy or the pain that went through her. Pink in the face, with love she called the girls who, afraid, had run under a cypress not far from the grave. She stopped crying, wiped a few tears that had escaped, and with a sweet and motherly tone, she smiled and said to them, "Come. Here is your father!"

The girls, zigzagging among the graves, ran happily toward them. Ermanno knelt and opened his arms. Flora and Laura came running and hugged him! The emotion was great, as was the hug of Ermanno. Then he got up and placed his hands on Marta's cheeks; he hugged her, kissed her, kissed her again, and she kissed him. In spite of the dirt stuck to the clothes and the rain that continued to fall, the four set off for the exit. The caretaker, at the entrance, was embarrassed when he saw two little girls holding an umbrella-like pouch on their heads, in the company of a lady hugging a man with a guitar slung across his back in the pouring rain.

Rocco stood at the entrance gate. With his hands on his hips he waited for the passage of that little family. Once he was close to her, he told Marta, "Did you come here for one reason, and leave with another? Do you intend to be with a stranger? I remind you that at 11 o'clock our wedding ceremony begins; you'd better hurry to get ready!" Marta, reassured by Ermanno's presence, replied, "He is my man. He fled because he did not know that I was pregnant. I had nightmares tonight. A sixth sense led me here, and to my surprise I saw him weeping near the grave on which it was written, 'La Cupa Ermanno. Fourteen years.'"

"What?" Rocco replied. "How you've changed in such a short time! What she said was bad, but the damage you did to us was worse."

Marta released the fear that for years she had held in her throat, and almost screaming, addresesd him in an aggressive voice, "You are a fake, an opportunist and a born slacker; a spy, you have always followed me in secret, and today you have done the same. Now you just have to disappear. Get lost."

After venting, Marta, the two little girls, and Ermanno crossed the cemetery gate.

Rocco, dismayed, remembered the words that Ermanno had thrown at him in the billiard room: "You will not marry her." Mortified, he bowed his head and realized that he had stepped on two pieces of colored glass: they were the lenses with which Ermanno had covered his pupils!

Maria Clara had shown her talent by contrasting the stone rabbit and the love story with today's tragic developments. In fact, the newspapers spoke of subversive groups that kidnapped people and sometimes even killed them, or of newborns thrown by their mothers into garbage bins. Faced with all this, what could a stone rabbit do if he did not move his reader? These thoughts crossed my mind immediately after I had finished reading the story, but the physical lack of Maria Clara tormented my heart.

To fill the void, I painted during the day and read by candlelight at night. In the meantime, I had not yet received any news about her because I had not registered my address at the town hall and so could not receive mail. The loneliness was so great that in order to calm myself I tried not to look at the calendar, but in my mind the thought of seeing Maria Clara as soon as possible was insistent.

One evening I went with the van to the village to pick up food, cigarettes, and old newspapers that the newsagent sold by weight. The latter I used to wrap the paintings to sell; some I read when the books bored me. Returning to the countryside under the darkness, I drove along dirt paths one after the other, and at one turn the headlights shone on two people who were struggling to try to defend themselves from a bunch of stray dogs. I stopped the van, and I beeped the horn, trying to scare the dogs away. Then I got out of the van leaving the headlights on, and with a stick found on the edge of the lane I rushed towards them. The strays, partly because of the light of the headlights and partly because I shook the stick at them, ran off barking and disappeared into the surrounding darkness.

"You shouldn't have moved, because you had nothing to defend yourself. In these cases, you have to have the strength to stand still, so the dogs can turn around and then slowly move away." At my words, those two people seemed to reassure themselves, and one shouted, "Sebastiano!" As I came closer they jumped on me with joy. It was Maria Clara and Lorenza, who at that hour, had walked to the estate after they had returned from their journey. We climbed into the van, and when I reached the estate's piazza, I parked; while the two women were heading toward the house, I set out to draw water from the well. With the bucket overflowing with fresh water, I entered the house, inviting Maria Clara and Lorenza to take a sip of water and wash their faces and to recover completely after the fright they had suffered.

The estate's owner, in view of the coming spring, had called a local farmer to prune the olive trees. He arrived early in the morning, around seven o'clock, on a bicycle upon whose handlebars he hung a wicker basket that held his tools. He did nothing to hide his distrust of us, and at the first opportunity he started talking so much that we hardly listened to him. He said that from what he had been able to see, we were parasites, and he accused us of this and that. For him, we, and all the people like us, were the cause of the social evil occurring in the country. He also confided to us that he had participated in the Liberation with the partisans, and that we, according to his judgment, were lazy, incapable of doing anything positive.

No doubt this man had risked his life for others. But that was another time. At least then they knew who they were fighting against. Today was a different story.

Then I told him, "Terrorism has no face. It is not us, and it is not people like us; the terrorists are the ones who go around bombing, jeopardizing the lives of all of us. The purpose of terrorism is to create demagogy. Its purpose is to destroy what you and we have helped to build: democracy. Underneath there is certainly something that's not working, someone who wants to destroy democracy. We, for our part, only want what we've earned. Do you think we are bothering anyone by being here? We work and don't go around begging or stealing. Work is a right for everyone, but not everyone works, because the right to work is just a purely theoretical fact, an article in this country's constitution. Many people in order to work are forced to kiss ass, which is precisely what the masters want. You, for example, who are retired, why do you keep working? Well, I think I can tell you: The pension you get is not enough for you to live. You have all your life paid taxes during your working years, and now? The bosses guaranteed you some extra money for overtime, while undercutting your fair salary to make cheaper products. Luckily you made it to retirement; others died before they could get there. This has happened to many who, while working hard, never lived to see it in their hands. What happened to their pension? Could be theirs was given to someone else who never worked a day in his life, and all this is thanks to the rotten corruption of civil society. They are the masters and parasites who have enriched themselves through the sweat of others and continue to get rich, impoverishing more and more the people who work. Of course, people who work and are poor are mad if our kind decides not to work. There's a sense of uneasiness that alienates the good and the beautiful. I mean, the habit of work has turned into a little madness, and you say that it is our fault. Bah!

"You elders believe that you always have reason on your side, while you live on old proverbs and let others solve your problems. Is it possible that you have not understood that everyone acts for his own benefit? In my opinion, it's always the poorest who get fucked in the ass, those who have the worst jobs. Straight-suited work, on the other hand, is reserved for court jesters and asslickers. This social scene has been going on for some time, and if I can understand it, it makes me angry to know that you don't. Not only that, you come here to break my balls with stupid moralism, with the speeches that others have driven into your head and believe it's all the truth. Fuck you."

"I'll going to tell the master, what you told me," the man replied, annoyed by my long speech. "I will also tell him," he added, "that you are revolutionary anarchists, and so I will drive you out of this place."

At this point, I wondered what this man could want from us and why he was so pissed off. I remember that the farmer, going away, cursed like an animal and kicked anything that happened to get in the way of his feet. As soon as the man disappeared, Maria Clara, who had witnessed the whole scene without uttering any words, burst out laughing and said, "He'll be back for sure; you'll see, he'll be back. Tomorrow he will come back with his tail between his legs to finish the work he has just begun."

She was right. The next day we found him in the trees, busy pruning. At noon, we invited him to have lunch with us. I struggled to convince him, and eventually he decided to join us. Breaking the ice was a bit embarrassing, due to the excitement of the previous day. His name was Vincenzo, and after introducing himself he asked us in a timid voice, "What do you do for a living?" We hesitated. He, this time, in a harsher tone, asked us once again, "What do you do?"

"Well, we try to spend as little as possible," Maria Clara replied.

"But money, how do you earn it?"

"Painting canvas," I replied as I invited him to follow me into the former stable used as a studio for my painting. Mastro Vincenzo scrutinized every single canvas with eyes full of wonder. Then, with a bit of amazement, he added, "You are artists! Do you know how much this gift of God is worth? You can become rich and famous."

With the voice of one who wanted to convince someone, I told him that I did not care about wealth, let alone becoming famous. I was content with what I could do. The important thing was that we made enough money to live. Mastro Vincenzo drank the coffee in one sip, lit a cigarette, and began to talk about himself and his problems, and said, "The biggest of my problems is my son Giorgio, who is confined to a wheelchair. He was twenty years old, and he didn't know what to do with his life. He was engaged and was willing to get married, but he hadn't learned a trade. One day he decided to enlist in the Public Security, one of the few makeshift ways for those who at twenty were without a job. One night he was on patrol on a highway. He did not even have time to tell them to halt when the bodies of his comrades collapsed to the ground, full of lead. He was the only survivor. His comrades died instantly, leaving their wives and children in the uncertain arms of tomorrow. Giorgio, in turn, was hit in several parts of the body. A bullet stuck in a disc of his spine. The various surgical procedures he underwent were useless. He left the hospital in a damn wheelchair, nailed there forever. Who was the culprit of all this? It is a question that still awaits an answer."

The eyes of master Vincenzo could hardly hold back the tears, which then slid down and furrowed his face. He got up suddenly, picked up his tools, and went to the field where other olive trees awaited him. Maria Clara and I realized we had gone a bit far the previous day, but there was no way we could know the drama that this man had been carrying within himself. Toward sunset, he finished pruning, gathered his things in the basket, and after saying goodbye, set the ladder under the canopy, headed to his bicycle, hung up the basket, mounted it, and pedaled away.

We felt bad as we watched him shrink as he moved away, until he disappeared behind a curve. Almost certainly Mastro Vincenzo was mulling that sad story to himself, hoping to find a glimpse of justice that would put an end to that drama, which by day stood at bay, only to follow him always the way home from work in the evening. Come to think of it, someone in those years had defined the children of '68 as "terrorists." The failed revolution had led a large number of privileged people down the wrong road. I think things got confusing because common criminals and delinquents had found their way into all the links of the movement of '68. Slogans such as "Make Love, not War," produced the opposite effect everywhere; the number of young people, in fact, who enlisted as mercenaries grew visibly. With the passage of time, the pacifists were marginalized. The false moralists were set with excellent salaries and consequently integrated into society. The anarchists, eternal intellectuals and excellent theorists, remained outside. Nobody would understand them inside the system. Once I had been one of them, and time has changed everything; it has changed me too, and now I am only a marginalized person. Years later, terrorist actions still occupy the main pages of newspapers.

Three days after having met Vincenzo and his drama, with the favor of the precocious spring climate, we loaded my canvases into the van and left for the feasts and festivals. After locking up the estate, we passed by Lorenza's house whom we had not seen for some time. Her mother told us that she was teaching in a provincial school as a substitute teacher until the end of the school year. Reluctantly we took the local road and then the state highway, traveling with the hope that we would sell some. We stopped at a place where a short-term exhibition was about to begin, and I participated, painting a scene of the local landscape. In the evening my picture was displayed with the others, and I felt bad because it didn't sell; in any case I managed to sell it a week later during a patronal feast.

We traveled around every day, and in the end I had no more canvases to show. Fortunately, it was already the beginning of September, and this convinced us to return home. On the way, Maria Clara, satisfied with the results of our long wandering for the festivals of the entire region, relaxed, listening to music from the headphones connected to the portable recorder playing the tapes she had purchased from the stalls. My music, on the other hand, was the roar of the engine, and I didn't listen to the tapes so as not to distract myself from driving. At noon, after having supplied ourselves with the necessities, we arrived in front of the columns of our estate. Maria Clara took the key from the empty dovecote and we went into the house. She opened doors and windows to ventilate the rooms that had been closed since the day we had left. A poster had been pasted on the kitchen wall that was not there before. It depicted the image of the Beatles walking on the street crossing of Abbey Road, immortalized on the cover of the album that took the street's name. On the stuffed chair, whose back rested against the wall, an envelope had been left next to the container of paint brushes, and Maria Clara opened it and then read the contents:

Hi, lovebirds

Lorenza and Sergio together with Marcella and her boyfriend Dario declare themselves guilty of having invaded your house, taking advantage of your unexpected absence. After traveling all over Europe and having bought this poster in London, they are back in Italy. We traveled through Italy in Dario's Jeep, and today, August 23, we passed by your estate to greet you. With the key taken from the dovecote, we entered the house. After seven hours of waiting, at sunset we were convinced that you two were off somewhere, running around with your green van. We hope to see you again soon; we greet you with affection.

Lorenza

P.S. In September I leave to teach outside the province.

"Too bad, they were here twenty days ago."

"It's nobody's fault; we'll see them next time," I replied, adding: "In exchange they left us a gift, this extraordinary poster of the Beatles."

Autumn arrived, and the countryside changed its appearance. Painting outdoors during the passing days became more and more difficult, due to an already strong wind which raised the dust from the still dry land near the estate. This often forced me to paint at home using acrylic colors to prevent the waft of oil and turpentine into the rooms. When I did not paint, I would break up pallets in order to get some boards, and I devoted myself to building a bookcase to be placed on a wall, cramming books in it that hung around all over the house.

Maria Clara, however, didn't pay attention to my work. She concentrated on listening to the radio and her audiocassettes, and when she was satisfied, in her hermitage, like an ascetic, she would collect herself and start writing. One day I saw her crying and I thought that it was because she wanted to publish and at the same time did not want to steal money from our savings. She was looking for a publisher who wouldn't ask for money to publish and doubted whether it could be possible. I also had doubts because patrons were a thing of the past. To give us courage, we often talked about things like that, and with loud music piercing our moods, we abandoned ourselves to love and erotic games. Our daily life for months remained in this menagerie, where we watched the vagaries of the weather and the gradual lengthening of daylight hours through the windows. Winter was packing its goodbye bags.

Once again, the beauty of spring returned. The first warm sun of March returned to shine on the winter-still countryside. The new air settled on the olive trees in the hills and then descended to the valley and finally dismantled the frost of February. Sudden showers from time to time justified the impertinence of March. The almond trees, already blooming, perfumed intensely, as did the cherry trees. The angel of the seasons watched over nature, lighting it with the colors of late spring, and rocked it with the wind, warmed it with the sun, and finally kissed it with rain. Maria Clara walked among the flowers, caught them with her eyes, caressed them, loved them, but left them where they were born. She let them die on the stalks, where the process of eternal change would take them. In that explosive green she loved to recite her poems. She was joyously screaming at the wind, then dropping down to rest and getting up with a start to get back running. She was happy and was shouting at me, saying: "Come, Elf of the woods! Leave the brushes for now. Let's take a ride to the old tower."

She ran like a deer, and I was having trouble keeping up with her. Then suddenly she slowed down as she reached the tower. The desire to make love in freedom grew wild in both of us, without restrictive formulae, and without masters to be respected. Our bodies were free, and they vibrated in sincere embraces and tender caresses. Free were our daydreams. Free flowed our talk, we held back nothing. What would happen to the world have if the rifles, spears, swords, axes, and molotovs were gone forever, and everyone learned to love instead of hate? Ah, we would certainly have at our fingertips what cosmic love is. Pain and sadness, if swept away from our hearts, would make us happy, because inside would be as if we had found God, Knowledge, and Consciousness. It would be wonderful if all the living beings of planet Earth definitively buried racism, praising universal brotherhood for eternity. I felt absurd during these mental games of mine. The blue of her eyes, on the other hand, was pure water, where I would sink and die, be reborn, and then go back to dying. I reflected on death, and I told myself that if Maria Clara's eyes were death, I had nothing to fear, I would have been safe in such a sweet eternity.

On a Tuesday in June I managed to get rid of the thick beard that I had grown during the winter. When I got to the barber, I was in a hurry to be shaved. However, I had to wait for my turn, and while waiting, started reading one of those weeklies that covered the table in the room, but which were always left where the customers sat. An international meeting of poetry and culture was reported in the main column from Thursday to Saturday at Castel Porziano, a location near ancient Ostia. Many critics and poets of international fame would be there. All this excited me so much that I wanted to report the news to Maria Clara, who in the meantime was busy enrolling in a driving course at a school authorized to grant licenses. As she was leaving, I told her about the news reported in the weekly. The new edition of the weekly magazine was published on Wednesday, and the barber let me take the page that interested me, so I read it to Maria Clara. The course she was supposed to attend began in twenty days, and reading in her face the desire to be there, I spontaneously told her: "Are we going to read some of ours?"

"Among all the poems I have written there is one that I would like to read in public. I really think I'd be happy to do that in Castel Porziano."

"Today is still Tuesday, we have the time to find out when the train leaves and to organize ourselves."

The train left at midnight every day and arrived at half past seven the following morning. We packed our bags. At about ten o'clock in the evening, on foot, we left the estate, heading for the train station. At half past seven, Thursday morning, we arrived in Rome. Then we took the subway to Ostia, and from there, the bus to Castel Porziano.

At one o'clock we ate lunch, and about two o'clock we headed for the beach that was to host the three evenings. It was immense, and the technicians worked hard to complete the assembly of the stage, the amplification, and the decorations. Meanwhile, the two of us looked around hoping to notice some known face. The sun hit hard, and we thought of taking a swim to cool off. We left our backpacks and sleeping bags near the stage and went down into the clear waters of the Tyrrhenian Sea. It was already four o'clock; tired by the long journey and the morning, we picked up our stuff from under the one side of the stage that had been finished by now. We sat on the sand between the backpacks and the sleeping bag and took a nap. When we woke up, a few meters from the center of the stage, the workers had mounted gazebos. Already they were filling up, so we sat on the ground, side by side. In this way a large human circle was forming, and the two of us completed a ring. There was about eighteen of us. Each of those present had already taken his book out of the baggage, reading its contents, and everyone listened in silence and with interest. One of the organizers murmured in our ear that if we wanted to read our work on stage, all we had to do was arrange it with the attendant who was not far away. Around 6:15 the reading for beginners began.

The poets took turns reading their verses at the microphone, the only figure on the stage where there were no chairs to prevent them from becoming blunt objects for some aggravation. Some laughed at the address of the declaimers, and others shouted severe criticism, but the poets did not allow themselves to be carried away by these impertinent acts. Maria Clara was no less so when she recited her "Song of the Winners:"

Human beings
Conquered by wars of hunger and famine.
Conquered by dogmas and taboos.
Victimized by cancer and atomic energy.
Human beings
Conquered by mafia and omertà,
from Gladio, and from the massacres of the State.
Conquered by Masons and the god of money.

Human beings
conquered by dictatorships
and false democracies,
by imbecility and arrogance.
Pushed flees
from everywhere
sealed in a big "00" flour sack.

Human beings
Conquered by usurers and suffocated by bills,
Conquered by inner conflicts
and by masks
that hide the moods.
Human beings
conquered by murders and suicides,
by morality, by plagiarism
and by racism.

Human beings
Conquered by bureaucracy and euphemisms like
"The law is equal for all."

Human beings
Conquered by image factories,
By journalists, writers and court poets.

Human beings
conquered by alcohol and nicotine,
by heroin and cocaine,
from the errors of calculation and regulation.

Human beings
so overcome by illusion
They jump on the winners' wagon.
This is the age of the vanquished
that to future memory

will deliver their stories.
of "false" winners,
but authentically true for the vanquished.

At the end, she came off the stage shaking; I welcomed her in my arms and said, "You were great!"

She only nodded, and together we mingled among the others to continue listening to the poets until the end. In the remaining time, and after several presentations on the spirit of the festival, and of those who had already published some books, began the performances of the pillars of the Beat Generation and other well-known poets.

The microphone was the master who dominated the scene. To our ears came cries as old as the centuries. The message was always the same. The deep search for the self, and the awareness of existence, and the battle against those who tried to suffocate us with the shroud of alienation. It was bad, this hiding under chameleon skin, pondering future traps for the hopes that each of us cultivated.

We all meditated upon the words we heard, processing thoughts in a capillary way. The evening came to an end, and we went to sleep, each slipping into his sleeping bag. The rain woke us in the early hours of the morning, forcing us to gather everything in a hurry to seek shelter under the stage. We found it crowded with people who were still sleeping. It was difficult, being tight like sardines, but we found a corner without disturbing anyone. Fortunately, the rain lasted only a few hours, then the sun, which rose imperiously, warmed our cold bodies. We left the last traces of goose bumps, walking away by the sea.

The second evening brought nothing new compared to the first. We tried to understand why the audience absolutely wanted the poets to echo the propaganda that some of the comrades had professed in their speeches. Almost all the ethnic groups on Earth were there with us, but they were nothing compared to the poets. Some in the audience tried to incite those present, to provoke the big shots with the goal of debunking the myths of poetry. All were silent, however, as soon as Allen Ginsberg took hold of the only microphone available on the stage. After his reading, others came on and the evening ended with a few fires on the beach and many left in the cold of the night. I couldn't close my eyes. All I did was roll in my sleeping bag, tormented by a thousand questions.

What was the meaning of that gathering? The goal was to bring poetry to the young masses, but these people had mocked the poets. What the fuck did they want from the poets? They had said much and done everything to advance poetry. Most people, perhaps, believed they had assimilated but had not understood that assimilating through books or the press was one thing, acting in full consciousness of certain situations was quite another. Many people wore long hair, but unlike their hair, their ideas were short, because everything was dictated by fashion trends. This was the bitter reality. Years ago, hair was grown in protest. Now there was nothing authentic about it. Most of the people attending had come just to be able to say in the future, "I was there too."

They did not give a damn about the poetry. The innocent ones, perhaps, were the poets. In that cluster of people, however, they ended up looking like freaks. I pondered these things, while Maria Clara seemed asleep, but in reality, she too was awake with her own her inner conflicts. Conscious both of not being able to sleep, our eyes, awake in agitation, spoke through implications. We left our sleeping bags. Then, without saying anything, we went for a walk. The night breeze enveloped us while we watched the warm glow of the small fires lit during the evening. The big stage had turned into a gloomy castle with the hippy guardians asleep under the now extinguished lights of the two side towers.

At that time of night, the beach was like a vast battlefield with dead and wounded strewn about in a theatrical performance. We walked for a long time, without saying a word. This silence was precious to us. Our eyes met with the same judgments about what we saw. Maria Clara, who stood beside me, paid attention to the meaning of my statements. Her eyes seemed to sink into the purity of silence, as if they wanted to speak to my heart. She fixed her gaze on me, and she was backlit with a sublime light. Her mouth opened to my kisses, and I pressed into her with all my strength. The connection was perfect; her face illuminated by splendid colors and full of joy. The embrace enveloped us; we melted, and our bodies lying on the sand, spread out.

Our eyes, pointing towards the sky, were immersed in the tranquility of that immense darkness. With serenity in our hearts, we thought of a better future. The night was still long on the horizon of the sea, and with our feet in the shallow water, along the shore, hand in hand, we walked aimlessly like two lovers dreaming of a future unhindered.

On the third day, tired and disappointed by the festival, we decided to return home. In the late afternoon we headed back to the city, and in Rome we boarded the train, which took us home by eight o'clock the next morning. After all, we thought we had touched the reality encountered at Castel Porziano, and that in some ways believed this experience would help us. Maria Clara above all was stimulated by the hope that among those people, there might have been some publisher. A month later a parcel was delivered in which there was an anthology of the emerging poets who had performed on that occasion, printed by the organization and sent to our address that was written on the back of the poem she had read. Maria Clara, proud and happy for that unexpected publication obtained without paying money, placed the book on our shelves and told me, "Now I too am in these volumes."

A cold and rainy winter kept us captive in the house, and we escaped now and then in our van. I accompanied Maria Clara in the village to her driving lessons until she got her license. Relieved at having obtained it, she resumed writing and I continued to paint as in the previous days. In spring we would follow the itinerary of the patronal festivals of the previous year. In September, however, the festival of Cosmo and Damian attracted us to the city of Trulli. In two days I sold all the paintings. It was Maria Clara who drove the van on the return journey of two hundred kilometers, not without a few mistakes, but overall, she did well, and we arrived home safely.

Two new things had happened. The first was she could now drive. The second, was that in October, I had to have surgery due to an ingrown toenail. Maria Clara was forced to drive the van every time I went to the clinic for the various medications. She, for her part, continued to apply for teaching jobs at the beginning of each school year.

We often received letters and postcards from Lorenza and Marcella, reflecting a firm friendship that bound us together. Meanwhile, Maria

Clara managed to print her own book at her own expense, and the booklet of poems was full of many modest truths, emptying her head of a grievance that had followed her like a ball and chain.

The new year began with heavy snowfall, forcing us to spend entire days glued to the fireplace. Fortunately for us, the wood piled up under the roof during the previous months lasted until the spring. Now, as usual, came the season we wandered for parties and festivals. This time in September we went to Ravenna in Romagna, where they had organized a Poetry Market. We arrived by train and Maria Clara rushed to pay to register as a reader, and also paid a fee to sell her printed poems. The event lasted only one day, and in the afternoon came the readings that continued until the evening. In the end, Maria Clara sold only a few copies, as did the others.

Times were changing. People were buying everything but books, and there were more writers than readers. Music concerts replaced the forums of films, TV series, and talk shows, and the singers had enough of a fan base to perform. In short, while the same period went well for them, it was a time of great disappointment for us. We promised to roll up our sleeves, to get busy, but actually we just vegetated.

On the morning of December 9th, the newspapers carried bad news. The musician and pacifist John Lennon, a former member of the Beatles, had been gunned down by several pistol shots at the entrance to the Dakota building. The killer was immediately arrested. The first rumors told of a fan who, with the excuse of an getting an autograph, approached and killed him.

Maria Clara and I talked about the news and we ended up saying that with that crazy act, the killer had created a myth. Life always revolved around the mistakes and tragedies, whether planned or random. It was no coincidence that this year in Italy there had been the massacre at the Bologna train station, and as usual, the authorities will never be able to capture those responsible for the killing. At most, they will feed the public with a packaged monster who knows where, slamming it on the front pages of the newspapers. So, what will happen in the future?

Winter and spring ended, and for us it did not change anything compared to other years except in August, when Maria Clara announced to me, between embarrassment and tenderness, that she was pregnant; I too was a bit embarrassed, after all, it's not every day I learn that I had generated a child. Aware of our future child, we cried together for joy, but thinking of what awaited us, we were overcome by the uncertainty, and a little fear started to baffle us. Maria Clara was making fun of me telling me that at the right time I caught myself reaching for the reverse gear, and I jokingly defended myself by telling her that she had too tightened her grip, leaving me with no escape. With these thoughts, we tried and succeeded in defusing the news by making ourselves strong and nurturing hopes for the years to come.

A dream occupied my mind:

We were in a shack, having dinner, when someone knocked on the door; I got up and went to see who it was. My woman's mother was calling me a delinquent who had made her daughter pregnant. Alice, however, appeared suddenly and urged us not to break down in the face of adversity; she asked me to tell her sister that she loved her and was happy for her nephew or niece, no matter the sex, because it only mattered that the baby be born healthy. My parents were also there; they had aged and that weight of their years was lighter than the misery that Maria Clara and I were living in; they urged us to make ourselves be heard.

In that drowsiness streamed other dreams:

Dazed, I could not close the door. A voice shouted at me not to leave her alone, to stand by her as I was responsible for her condition, and to caress her belly to feel the vibrations of life. The fetus loves cuddles. Maria Clara urged me to look at her face; in pain I opened my eyes to see her weeping; I stroked her long hair and hugged her tightly to me, weeping, her head bent over my shoulder. For the first time I saw her face; she had faced many situations without ever yielding to fear and uncertainty; her eyes seem to kneel in front of the pain that, perhaps, would soon be alive again. I tenderly kissed her cheeks and drank her tears: sweet, sour, and salty. I glued my mouth to hers; my hands went down her sides, until I caught the warmth there, between her wonderful legs. Could you give me voice? My flesh in her flesh, and I sighed deeply as we gathered our senses. She, however, stopped me to say: "You will leave, and I will not be able to do anything to stop you. I would like you to stay with me forever, but you ... you will still leave, and leave me alone."

I replied that I would never leave her, even if misery crushed us. I couldn't understand what had destroyed our relationship.

I turned on the water but nothing came out. We rushed toward the well and lowered the bucket. We pulled it up quickly, but it was empty. Misery! I exclaimed. Our thirst grew. I started screaming like crazy. I was desperate when I felt her grab my hands.

"What happened?" I said to Maria Clara, and she, surprised, said, "You woke up? You were screaming about some danger. Did you have a nightmare? The next time you drink wine, you'd better not drink so much."

I recalled then the story Maria Clara had won for the "Poems and Tales Against the War" contest.

The shot

Giovanni was a writer who did not follow fashion. He wrote what he felt. The things he wrote offered him only moral satisfaction and nothing more, although he wanted to make money. The money he hoped to get was not for him, but for his daughters Lucia, Sonia, and Domenica.

Years ago, his wife had left him. She was tired of living with a starving man, who traveled about, trying to sell his poems and stories, earning barely enough to survive. He had not seen her since. Tired of wandering far and wide, he returned to his country. His parents, who had been dead for some time, had left him a beautiful farmhouse surrounded by woods. Giovanni, finding nothing else, went to live there with his three daughters. The years passed quickly. He had managed to find work as proofreader in a print shop. The three daughters, now grown up, worked in a tailor shop. For some time, however, Giovanni had problems with his health, and when he got worse, after the usual hospital visits, they told him that he had to undergo surgery for which they needed some blood. The blood bank needed donors. The day before the surgery, Lucia, Sonia, and Domenica asked their employer for a day off, and early in the morning they went to the transfusion center and donated blood.

Back home, they had breakfast, and not thinking about the fate of their father, each one looked for something to do. Sonia and Domenica devoted themselves to straightening up the house. Lucia thought of going into the woods to look for mushrooms. She was not a talented gatherer, and looking into the basket, she realized that it was not worth zigzagging through the bushes. Among other things, without realizing it, she had traveled a good stretch of road. A sharp thud echoed in the woods.

Lucia bent her knees as if she were to genuflect in front of a sacred icon, trying to remove the brambles with her hands, but the intense green of the sticker burrs invaded her eyes. Soon the music got louder, opening the windows of her last vision: John Lennon had left the Beatles and was headed her way.

He looked at her, and said, "What are you doing here dressed like that?"

"I'm looking for mushrooms."

"You're looking for them in the wrong place," John replied and added, "Look around you; we're in a strawberry field."

Lucia found it hard to keep her eyes open. She saw that the strawberry field, beaten by an unusual hail, had turned into a red mud, and on the horizon was a wall where two canvases were hung. One was the "Guernica" by Pablo Picasso, and the other the "Sunflowers" by Vincent Van Gogh, who with their heads bowed, had already cried for the victims of the wars. Faced with such a scenario, she half-closed his eyes, and a song rose:

"There was a guy who, like me, loved the Beatles and the Rolling Stones."

The rhythms and words of this song shook her and opened her eyes, she looked at John and said, "What are you doing here? As far as I know, you died, several years ago."

"You're kidding!" John replied, rebuking her.

"Not at all," Lucia replied a little resentfully, adding: "One of your fans killed you with a gun, unloading the whole magazine. The news was on television, and we saw your fans singing your songs, including the most beautiful one you ever wrote, 'Imagine.'

"Listen, I never wrote any song with that title," John continued, quite surprised, "and if you've listened to it, you certainly know the lyrics, and so I ask you to sing at least one refrain."

"Of the song, however, I know the title and a few words. Daddy was, in the past, a fervent admirer of you; he knows all your songs."

"It doesn't matter; what you remember is fine."
Lucia began to sing and the notes jumped from branch to branch:
'Imagine that all people live in peace.
Imagine that there is no hell and no heaven
that there is only heaven on earth.
It's easy if you try ...'
Sorry John, but I do not remember anything else."
Lucia was silent, and John took the song up where she interrupted him. Shortly thereafter, absolute silence fell! Meanwhile, Sonia and Domenica, not seeing Lucia return, decided to go and look for her in the woods. They looked between the cliffs and the thick tree-lined planes; they screamed loudly when they noticed her among the holly bushes intertwined with the brambles, and under a young oak tree. She seemed to be asleep. They called her; then turned her toward them, and saw a rose of blood on her chest. There were screams, desperation, crying out loud, senseless emotional gestures and a tension that made the leaves of the trees vibrate. Sonia, sobbing, slipped the earphone from her ears, took it to hers, pressed the keys of the tape player, and began to listen:
"Imagine that all people live in peace ...!" Turning to Domenica, she said:
"She was listening to songs about peace."
"Yeah!" She added, with amazement, "in the meantime some abominable being has passed through here, who thought he was at war."

After receiving the prize for her collection, Maria Clara and I left the room and walking around the village noticed a poster of a musical event in the dialect of Salento. The concert was scheduled for 9:30, in about half an hour, so we calmly visited the city monuments, and then we met again in the square where the event began.

The group that performed was called "Quelli della Taranta," and they played with an accordion, four girls singing with tambourines, and two guitars. Everyone danced the *pizzica* under the stage, even the children were dragged in. We were roasting sausages, and many drank wine until we were tired, and in this whirlwind of emotion we were both drawn, sinking into that liberating dance. With the excuse of toasting Maria

Clara's prize, I drank a few more glasses, and the consequence was that I fell asleep on the seat while she drove the truck through flat lands. At a rest stop I went to the bathroom, drank a coffee, and completely refreshed myself, I felt able to take over driving the van. After refueling, I drove us back home.

All that had happened later, as Maria Clara had recounted. I was in a hospital bed, still as a salami, my head in a daze. I saw only murky, elusive shadows. I felt as though people were holding down my arms, but I couldn't figure out why. When I regained consciousness I began to understand what had happened.

Maria Clara cried without sound. Her wide eyes were like lightning in the darkness. "Where are we?" I asked hoarsely.

"At the hospital," she answered in a soft, subtle voice to avoid frightening me.

"How long have I been like this?"

"For about twenty days. Do you remember? We had just come out of the publisher's office, where nothing happened, and near the station you were struck by a sudden illness, collapsed on the ground and vomited blood. I shouted for help."

I couldn't figure out why she was crying. The operation seemed to have been successful, so why was she in tears. Maybe it hadn't gone well. Had the doctors fooled us? Was I on my way out? We humans are made like this. We always think of the worse when we are well. While the wound was healing, I was still in pain. I couldn't hear over the noise of the doctors there. They were using technical language that I didn't understand; however one word they kept repeating was "metastasis."

What did that word mean? Boh! Here everyone answered in a cordial but evasive manner. One thing was certain: Autumn was here and I was terribly sick. Maria Clara had to help me get from my bed to the bathroom and had to hold me for my short walks in the hallway. I noticed that her belly grew bigger.

For several days I had been suffering ever more intense pains. I could not describe how much I suffered. The nurse was punctual with my sedative. Tonight I will be able to sleep thanks to that vial. The small radio on the bedside table announced the horoscope of the day. Then followed an old Beatles song, "Eleanor Rigby." That old song brought back memories of when I was bedridden with bronchitis, and my bedside radio had played the same song. How old am I? How many things haven't I accomplished; how many dreams have I not achieved? How much sadness and affliction, melancholy and bitterness remained inside! I realized that I was beginning to change; I was no longer myself. Perhaps I had never been. I no longer understood myself. I did not understand these memories, which came and went in my thoughts!

I asked Maria Clara to buy me a notebook so I could spend my time jotting down some memories. She brought me a notebook and pen, and when I could, I started writing about my misfortunes. On the first page I wrote: "To Maria Clara with the purest of feelings."

It was a Saturday evening in April 1970, and spring had not completely appeared.

Sometime later, one morning around noon, a postman stopped by. Looking toward the threshing floor, as was his custom, he saw a little girl running after geese and hens, and heard a voice calling out, "Irene, come and have breakfast, and then you can come back to play."

Nearby, under a canopy, a man was intent on painting a canvas on his easel. A little further on, a green van was parked. On the windshield there was a sign with two announcements: "We perform carpentry work at home. For any contacts, call 080..." and "High school graduate gives after-school classes to pupils and students. For information, call 080..."

"Daddy, Mommy, the postman is here," said the girl.

Maria Clara appeared at the door and noticed the man standing near the scooter, approached him and saw that he had a large envelope in his hand.

"You have to sign the receipt," said the postman. Maria Clara hurried to sign it. The postman started his scooter and took off.

"Sebastiano, come here; there's a letter for you from the hospital," she yelled. Inside the envelope were two short letters.

Dear Mr. Sebastiano Ferrara,

We hope you will take advantage of the therapy prescribed for you on your discharge papers. We wish you a brief and successful convalescence and remind you that our facility is at your disposal for every need.

In wishing you a brief and correct convalescence, I remind you that our facility is at your disposal for any need.

N.B. I remind you that you need to return for the first check-up in six months.

Sincerely,
Gianluca Tivoli, Professor of Primary Care

The second one read:

Dear Mr. Sebastiano Ferrara

As you requested, enclosed are the photocopies of your medical record. Having fulfilled the responsibilities of our services, we ask that you return the release form in the postage paid envelope enclosed.

Regards
Riccardo Riuta, Manager
Health Administration

Sebastiano and Maria Clara looked at each other, and she said: "See how quick our postal service is? The letter took only four years to get here, as the stamp clearly shows. If you really had had cancer, it would have eaten you away by now!"

They looked deeply into each other's eyes.

Irene, who, feeling neglected, demanded her mother's attention, asking for breakfast. Sensing her presence, her parents drew her into their hug, and their tears joined hers.

AFTERWORD

"It was a Saturday evening in April, one thousand nine hundred and seventy ... and spring had not yet fully arrived...." The beginning, which is also found in the end of the novel, tells us Sebastiano is in the hospital writing down his story in a notebook, and at a concert of PFM where he meets Maria Clara. They will meet each other again in a month's time at the next concert, the Nomads and Guccini. Meanwhile, Sebastiano recounts his life through memories. The memories flow through his mind like a train running on a dead track, and they will be interrupted by the chaos of a concert or by the encounter that awaits its inevitable destiny: Maria Clara.

Sebastiano first presents it to us and then gives her a direct voice, beside her as she speaks in the first person. It is an act of mutual love, as if to say that he and Maria Clara achieve a true equality of man and woman. It is a beautiful effect, one that introduces a new way of seeing the working relationship between a couple, which today is still in crisis. Each of us can learn to see choices and ways of living by reading the love story between Sebastiano and Maria Clara.

After lightning strikes, the two meet again at a concert and together journey through the thunder and rains of dangerous storms that flood events until they flow over the banks of the drama. The thunders are the obstacles and difficulties caused by the inner and outer pains that each face. After the deluge comes the sunshine of love that makes the simple times they share fertile and flourishing.

The two protagonists wrap themselves in the myth of the Beatles, along with other songwriters, books, and everything that is part of the Beat Generation movement. Prejudices, rumors, erotic games, resentments, and weariness will clash with the pretentiousness of ecclesiastical, scholarly authoritarianism and daily life condensed on the walls of usury, blackmail, bribes, illegal abortions, and other dangers. Among these behaviors of the so-called civil society will appear two female figures as focal characters of the entire work, and who will express, wrongly or rightly, the elements that generate the fate of the two protagonists.

On the one hand, there are the ambitions and intrigues of a bourgeois like the mother of Maria Clara with her practicing clandestine abortions and being always on the side of the winners in power (in contradiction with the national feminist movement which is joined by Maria Clara and her friend and colleague Lorenza). On the other, there is Sara, Sebastiano's fiancée, who at the point of marrying, betrays him for another. Her ambitions, in fact, were those of many young women of the time: her husband's luxury car, money to buy magazines and fashionable clothes, unbridled fun and behaviors incited by television programs. These are the two female stereotypes of the South of Italy, a collection of social, political, and behavioral thunders that precede the advent of a consumerism that threatens to brings all minds to the same level.

Those who suffer include Sebastiano and Maria Clara who will learn to live together, surviving thanks to the money obtained from the peddling of his paintings and her private lessons to students. With these two sources of livelihood, their drama will result in the birth of their daughter Irene, and Sebastiano's overcoming the shocking diagnosis of a suspected cancer requiring a long hospital stay. The behavior of two focal characters will emerge and form the events that the two lovers play as protagonists.

One behavior is that of the mother of Maria Clara who forces her daughter to leave home, and the other is the betrayal and abandonment of Sebastiano by Sara. The mother who is a practicing obstetrician, and Sara who works as a knitter in a clothing company, are the two crucial elements that will decide the fate of the two protagonists. After all, there will be the copious and stormy rains that will fall on them. The rains will fall on him in a village, and on her in a city, showing that in reality what happens in the country also happens in the city. These two characters suggest that in the purity of events, what goes unseen, good and evil, are interdependent, they are an interaction, and as such, they are the foundation of all historical sources in their ethical aspects.

The two protagonists rent an estate. Here they will live their best days, including trips to patron saint celebrations hoping to sell some paintings, and those to Castel Porziano or Ravenna, where Maria

Clara will be appreciated for her style and her creativity as a writer. Both painter and writer travel only with their talent, learning from newspapers and radio such news as the death of John Lennon and the succession of wars that divide public opinion only to be soon forgotten.

Puzzle is also the words of denunciation of those who have no voice in history, those left out of history who fight for their lives. The fertility and energy of the two protagonists will survive Sebastiano's illness and Maria Clara's giving birth to new life. At this point, after the repetition of the beginning, the ending is told as if to point out that the future belongs to a third person. This third person who appears on the scene is her daughter Irene. It is she, perhaps, who begins to tell her life from her first steps: *"A moment later, Maria Clara felt a tugging at her skirt. It was Irene, who, feeling neglected, demanded her mother's attention, asking for her breakfast. Sensing her presence, her parents drew her into their hug, and their tears joined hers."*

Donato Caputo

ABOUT THE AUTHOR

SANTE CANDELORO was born and lives in Castella Grotte, Provincia di Bari, in the region of Puglia. He is retired from a career in hospital nursing. Throughout his life he has written poetry and stories that have been published in local magazines. His book publications include *Versi di Versi*, a collection of his poetry, and *Puzzle*. Candeloro is also an accomplished painter and furniture maker.

ABOUT THE TRANSLATOR

FRED L. GARDAPHÉ is Distinguished Professor of English and Italian American Studies at Queens College and the John D. Calandra Italian American Institute of the City University of New York. He has published monographs in the field of Italian American studies, as well as journalism, fiction and poetry. His previous translations include Claudia Donadoni's play, *Stria*, performed in the 2018 edition of the *In Scena* Italian theater festival in New York, and poetry by Lawrence Ferlinghetti, Luigi Fontanella, and Augusto Lentricchia.

CROSSINGS
AN INTERSECTION OF CULTURES

Crossings is dedicated to the publication of Italian-language literature and translations from Italian to English.

Rodolfo Di Biasio. *Wayfarers Four*. Translated by Justin Vitello. 1998. ISBN 1-88419-17-9. Vol 1.

Isabella Morra. *Canzoniere: A Bilingual Edition*. Translated by Irene Musillo Mitchell. 1998. ISBN 1-88419-18-6. Vol 2.

Nevio Spadone. *Lus*. Translated by Teresa Picarazzi. 1999. ISBN 1-88419-22-4. Vol 3.

Flavia Pankiewicz. *American Eclipses*. Translated by Peter Carravetta. Introduction by Joseph Tusiani. 1999. ISBN 1-88419-23-2. Vol 4.

Dacia Maraini. *Stowaway on Board*. Translated by Giovanna Bellesia and Victoria Offredi Poletto. 2000. ISBN 1-88419-24-0. Vol 5.

Walter Valeri, editor. *Franca Rame: Woman on Stage*. 2000. ISBN 1-88419-25-9. Vol 6.

Carmine Biagio Iannace. *The Discovery of America*. Translated by William Boelhower. 2000. ISBN 1-88419-26-7. Vol 7.

Romeo Musa da Calice. *Luna sul salice*. Translated by Adelia V. Williams. 2000. ISBN 1-88419-39-9. Vol 8.

Marco Paolini & Gabriele Vacis. *The Story of Vajont*. Translated by Thomas Simpson. 2000. ISBN 1-88419-41-0. Vol 9.

Silvio Ramat. *Sharing A Trip: Selected Poems*. Translated by Emanuel di Pasquale. 2001. ISBN 1-88419-43-7. Vol 10.

Raffaello Baldini. *Page Proof*. Edited by Daniele Benati. Translated by Adria Bernardi. 2001. ISBN 1-88419-47-X. Vol 11.

Maura Del Serra. *Infinite Present*. Translated by Emanuel di Pasquale and Michael Palma. 2002. ISBN 1-88419-52-6. Vol 12.

Dino Campana. *Canti Orfici*. Translated and Notes by Luigi Bonaffini. 2003. ISBN 1-88419-56-9. Vol 13.

Roberto Bertoldo. *The Calvary of the Cranes*. Translated by Emanuel di Pasquale. 2003. ISBN 1-88419-59-3. Vol 14.

Paolo Ruffilli. *Like It or Not*. Translated by Ruth Feldman and James Laughlin. 2007. ISBN 1-88419-75-5. Vol 15.

Giuseppe Bonaviri. *Saracen Tales*. Translated by Barbara De Marco. 2006. ISBN 1-88419-76-3. Vol 16.

Leonilde Frieri Ruberto. *Such Is Life*. Translated by Laura Ruberto. Introduction by Ilaria Serra. 2010. ISBN 978-1-59954-004-7. Vol 17.

Gina Lagorio. *Tosca the Cat Lady*. Translated by Martha King. 2009. ISBN 978-1-59954-002-3. Vol 18.

Marco Martinelli. *Rumore di acque*. Translated and edited by Thomas Simpson. 2014. ISBN 978-1-59954-066-5. Vol 19.

Emanuele Pettener. *A Season in Florida*. Translated by Thomas De Angelis. 2014. ISBN 978-1-59954-052-2. Vol 20.

Angelo Spina. *Il cucchiaio trafugato*. 2017. ISBN 978-1-59954-112-9. Vol 21.

Michela Zanarella. *Meditations in the Feminine*. Translated by Leanne Hoppe. 2017. ISBN 978-1-59954-110-5. Vol 22.

Francesco "Kento" Carlo. *Resistenza Rap*. Translated by Emma Gainsforth and Siân Gibby. 2017. ISBN 978-1-59954-112-9. Volume 23.

Kossi Komla-Ebri. *EMBAR-RACE-MENTS*. Translated by Marie Orton. 2019. ISBN 978-1-59954-124-2. Volume 24.

Angelo Spina. *Immagina la prossima mossa*. 2019. ISBN 978-1-59954-153-2. Volume 25.

Luigi Lo Cascio. *Otello*. Translated and edited by Gloria Pastorino. 2020. ISBN 978-1-59954-158-7. Volume 26.

www.ingramcontent.com/pod-product-compliance
Lightning Source LLC
Chambersburg PA
CBHW020022030726
47499CB00007B/2224